The
by the

Dylid
y dyddia

————
————
————
————
————
————
————
————
————
————
————
————

A GATHERING
of GIANTS

*For my mum and dad, neither of whom
have ever been kidnapped by Giants. Yet.*

Published 2022 by Macmillan Children's Books
an imprint of Pan Macmillan
The Smithson, 6 Briset Street, London EC1M 5NR
EU representative: Macmillan Publishers Ireland Ltd, 1st Floor,
The Liffey Trust Centre, 117–126 Sheriff Street Upper
Dublin 1, D01 YC43
Associated companies throughout the world
www.panmacmillan.com

ISBN 978-1-5290-4698-4

Text copyright © Cat Weldon 2022
Illustrations copyright © Katie Kear 2021

The right of Cat Weldon and Katie Kear to be identified as the author
and illustrator of this work has been asserted by them in accordance
with the Copyright, Designs and Patents Act 1988.

1 3 5 7 9 8 6 4 2

A CIP catalogue record for this book is available from the British Library.

Printed and bound by CPI Group (UK) Ltd, Croydon CR0 4YY

•HOW TO BE A• HERO

A GATHERING of GIANTS

CAT WELDON

Illustrated by Katie Kear

MACMILLAN CHILDREN'S BOOKS

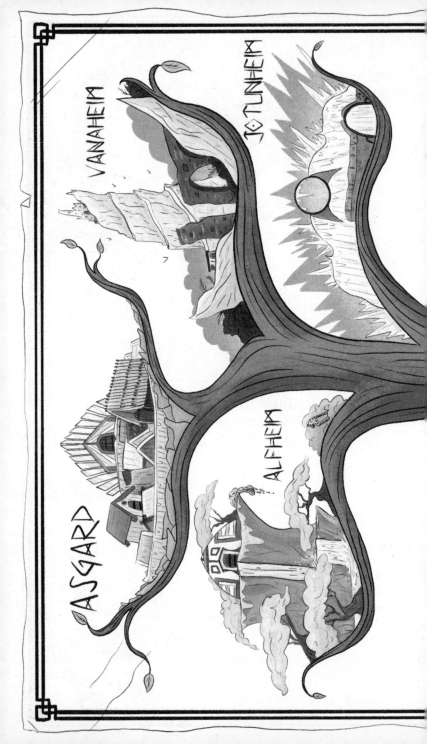

A Guide to the Nine Worlds
By Blood-Runs-Cold, Leader of the Valkyries

The Nine Worlds

Imagine the biggest tree you can. No, bigger than that.

BIGGER.

BIGGER.

That's Yggdrasil, and it makes your tree look like a bit of wilted broccoli. Nine whole worlds hang from Yggdrasil – *that's* how big it is.

Asgard: Right at the top, because it's the best. Home of the Gods and ruled over by Odin. In Asgard you can find *Valhalla*, Odin's Great Hall, where the greatest warriors come after they've died. There they can fight, feast and drink until *Ragnarok*, the battle at the end of the world. At Ragnarok they will be called upon to fight the Frost Giants for Odin, but until then it's basically party time.

Vanaheim: Home to the Gods who aren't cool enough to be in

Asgard. They're mostly interested in growing stuff; inhabitants of Asgard are more interested in fighting.

Alfheim: Home of the Elves. Yes, they have pointy ears. Yes, they giggle a lot. Mostly harmless, but keep them where you can see them.

Jotunheim: Home of the Giants, including our mortal enemies the Frost Giants. They keep trying to break into Asgard; we keep beating them in battle. Lots of mountains; good for skiing.

Midgard: This is where you can find living humans, living their ordinary lives, with ordinary horses, ordinary farms and ordinary families.

Svartalfheim: Home of the Dwarves. A maze of caves and mines. They love tinkering with gold and making magical gadgets.

Muspell: Land of Fire. Ruled over by Sutr, a Fire Giant. Nice saunas.

Helheim: Home of the Queen of the Dead, Hel. Yes, she named the place after herself. Tells you everything you need to know, really.

Niflheim: Land of the Unworthy Dead. The dragon Nidhogg

lives here and chews on the roots of the world tree. He likes poetry, gold and trampling anyone unlucky enough to be sent there.

Who's Who in Asgard

Odin: The Allfather, the Spear Shaker, the Terrifying One-Eyed Chief of the Gods. The boss.

Frigg: Goddess of Family. Odin's wife. Knows the future, but won't tell anyone.

Loki: The Trickster. Enjoys a 'joke'. Approach with caution. Technically a Fire Giant, but Odin lets him live in Asgard because they're blood brothers.

Thor: God of Thunder. Do not touch his hammer. Seriously.

Freyja: Goddess of Love and Sorcery. Likes cats. *I'm not kidding about the cats. She has cat ornaments, cat jewellery, and is usually covered in cat hair. She even has a pair of giant cats for pulling her chariot.*

Freyr: God of Summer and Freyja's brother. Loves a party, he's got the moves!

The Valkyries: Elite female warriors, Valkyries are servants of Odin, Chief of the Gods. They bring the greatest warriors and

Heroes to Valhalla on their flying horses. At Ragnarok, the battle at the end of the world, they will lead the Gods and warriors of Valhalla in the final clash against the Frost Giants.

Travel between Worlds

It is possible to travel between worlds by flying or climbing through Yggdrasil's branches. Not easy, but possible. Only the Gods (and Valkyries) have really got the hang of it. The Giants have managed it a few times, more through luck than anything else.

Valkyries and Odin travel by flying horse, Loki has special shoes, and Freyja uses a magic cloak. The Bifrost Bridge links Asgard and Midgard. When humans on Midgard see it, they call it a rainbow.

Magic

It's simple: magic can only be created by magical creatures – Dwarves, Elves and, to a certain extent, Giants. All other magic comes from magical objects *made* by magical creatures, usually the Dwarves.

Except for Odin: he learned how to do magic by hanging upside down from Yggdrasil for nine days to discover the secrets of the Runes. Fancy doing that? No? Then no magic for you.

Chapter One

A Birthday to Remember

'I look ridiculous!'

Whetstone peered at himself in the polished bronze mirror. His reflection was a bit wobbly and blurred, but he could see enough. That was the thing about staying with Freyja, the Goddess of Love and Sorcery: there were plenty of reflective surfaces. 'I feel like an idiot.' He pushed the feather, which stuck out of his hat, away from his eye. Gone were his scruffy clothes with their familiar holes and patches, replaced by . . . *this*.

Lotta's face contorted as she forced down a grin. 'It's not *that* bad.'

Whetstone twirled around. The sky-blue woollen tunic and leather belt were all right, even if the fur trim itched against his neck. But the trousers were just stupid. Big and baggy with green and white stripes, they ballooned out around his legs before being pulled in tight just below his knees. Strips of fabric wound snugly around his calves to finish the look. Lotta's eyes bulged as she tried not to laugh.

'I don't see why Freyja won't let us wear our own clothes,' Whetstone grumped, tightening his belt, worried his saggy breeches might slip down at any moment.

'Because we're fugitives in Asgard and we don't want anyone to recognize us?' Lotta suggested. Asgard was Home of the Gods and a very dangerous place for a living human and disgraced trainee Valkyrie to be hiding.

'Recognize YOU, you mean. No one knows me!' Whetstone pouted. 'Why do I have to look like a fool?'

'Yeah, no one knows you – except most of the Valkyries, and Loki, and—'

'Loki isn't back in Asgard yet.'

'*Yet.*' Lotta nudged Whetstone out of the way of the mirror. Instead of her usual leather and armour, she was wearing a pair of loose silk trousers and an embroidered tunic that contrasted perfectly with her brown skin, her black hair tucked neatly away beneath a patterned head wrap. She scratched at her head. 'I can't decide if it's a good thing he's not back yet, or if it just means he's planning something really bad.'

The last time Whetstone and Lotta had seen Loki, he'd tracked them to Helheim, one of the most miserable places in the Nine Worlds.

'*And* you didn't have to have a B A T H,' Whetstone muttered, his skin looking pinker and cleaner than it had in a long time. The feather flicked back into his eye. 'I can't think of many things worse than a bath.'

Behind them, a string of bunting was hoisted up towards

the gold domed ceiling. '*I* can't believe Freyja is actually going ahead with this party,' Lotta muttered, straightening her tunic.

'It's her birthday – it would look weird if she didn't,' Whetstone replied, stepping out of the way of a servant boy unenthusiastically pushing a broom across the floor.

Party preparations continued around them. Rich tapestries and brightly woven fabrics decorated the walls of Freyja's Great Hall. A long table had been pushed to one side and clusters of chairs were dotted around the space. Another servant scampered about, lighting clay lamps.

A very large and fluffy brown cat watched the servants scurry to and fro, his eyes on the bowls of nibbles they carried. With a leap, the cat landed on the long table, sending plates and glasses flying. Whetstone dashed across the room, snatching up the cat around its middle.

'Stop it, Mr Tiddles. You're going to get in trouble.'

The cat gave Whetstone a grumpy look as the boy carried him across the room to his bed of plump cushions. Lotta pinched her nose as they passed to try and hold back a sneeze. She was *explosively* allergic to cats.

With a screech that almost made Whetstone drop Mr Tiddles, a coppery falcon swooped into the room. In a ripple of light, the falcon transformed into Freyja, the birthday girl herself. A vision in silks and gold, she unfastened a feathery cloak and handed it to a waiting servant. Her magic necklace gleamed against the brown skin of her throat. She turned to Whetstone and Lotta. 'There you two are!'

Whetstone dropped Mr Tiddles on to his cushion and

moved to face her, his bottom lip sticking out. He gestured at his clothes. 'Why? Why would you make me wear this?'

Freyja straightened the feathery plumes on his hat. 'You're hiding in plain sight. The last place anyone would think to look for you is with the musicians.'

Lotta let out a snort of laughter.

'Musicians?' Whetstone spluttered. 'But I'm not musical: I can't play any instruments or anything!'

'It's simple. Just hang around at the back of the group and look busy.' Freyja handed him a narrow wooden harp.

Whetstone took it sourly. 'A harp? You think you're funny, don't you?'

Whetstone's problems had begun when he and his parents had got in the way of Loki stealing a magic harp from the Dwarves. The Dwarves had cursed the harp strings, hiding them in separate worlds so that Loki would be unable to use their power. As Whetstone and his parents had been holding the strings at the time, they were also taken and separated. Now Loki was hunting down the missing harp strings, not to reunite Whetstone's broken family or to make amends for his theft, but to use the powers they contained. Odin had set Whetstone the quest of collecting the strings before Loki could find them. A quest that had led them across several of the Nine Worlds before finally ending up here – at Freyja's birthday party.

Lotta bit her lip. 'Freyja, are you sure this is a good idea? Most of Asgard is coming to this party. Maybe we should just hide somewhere.' Her fingers twisted together nervously. 'We've been lucky so far, but someone is bound to notice us sooner or later.'

'No way!' Whetstone spluttered. 'I've been looking forward to this. If I have to spend another day quietly reading in Freyja's library, I'm going to go nuts.'

'We've been researching to try and figure out how to rescue your mum and break the curse!' Lotta countered.

'No, *I've* been researching the curse; *you've* been looking up Valkyries with magic powers. I saw you,' Whetstone retorted.

Lotta twisted an escaped curl between her fingers. 'I was just curious about what happened to me,' she muttered, avoiding his eyes. Lotta had returned from their trip to Helheim with her shield, a new sword and some very *unusual* powers. Some were useful, like the ability to melt the scary inhabitants of Helheim. Others . . . not so much, like blasting fire or feathers every time she sneezed.

'Well, all that reading has got us no further.' Whetstone crossed his arms. 'We need a new plan. If we keep our ears open at the party, we might hear something useful.'

'Plus, you'll be safer out in the open.' Freyja picked up a platter of tiny sandwiches. 'My last party got a bit out of control. I found Thor snoring in my wardrobe the next morning.'

Lotta crossed her arms.

'It will be fine.' Freyja pushed the sandwiches into Lotta's arms. 'Just keep busy and no one will notice a thing.'

❋

Lotta ducked through the crowd, trying to avoid catching anyone's eye, her tiny sandwiches already having been demolished by Thor in one massive mouthful. A table covered with birthday presents sat off to one side, most of them wrapped in gold paper. Lotta dawdled in front of them.

Pretending to be Freyja's waitress was *exhausting*. All of Asgard had come to the party, except for the two people she most wanted to see – Odin, Chief of the Gods, and Scold, ex-Leader of the Valkyries.

Lotta was a trainee Valkyrie, or, rather, she had been. She wasn't quite sure what she was any more. Valkyries were elite female warriors, brought to life by the breath of Odin and given the task of collecting fallen Heroes and warriors from the battles of Midgard, the human world. Unfortunately, on her first visit to Midgard, Lotta had accidentally picked up Whetstone, a very-much-alive apprentice thief instead of a dead warrior. It was only after Whetstone had proved he was a Hero by defeating a dragon that Odin had allowed Lotta to continue with her Valkyrie training. But that had all happened while Scold was in charge. Things were very different with the Valkyries now.

A conga line led by Freyr, the God of Summer, danced past Lotta. Freyr was Freyja's brother, his blond hair bright against his dark brown skin. 'La, la, la, la, la, hey!' the dancers chanted, looping around the hall and scooping up more people.

Lotta shuffled the birthday gifts around. Cat ornaments, mugs with cat ears and cat-shaped jewellery appeared under her distracted fingers.

Whetstone had vanished into the group of musicians, all dressed in identical feathery hats and sky-blue robes. Lotta wondered what he'd told them to explain why he couldn't play the harp he was holding. Maybe they didn't care. No one seemed to have noticed that Whetstone wasn't glowing like the other inhabitants of Asgard either, so maybe Freyja had performed some magic to keep him safe.

Lotta straightened her shoulders. She *should* go back to the kitchen for more tiny sandwiches before anyone got suspicious. Instead, she pushed a few more presents into line. A stout, gold object peeked out from behind a collection of paw-print bath towels.

Lotta sucked in a breath, her heart racing. 'Oh no, not you!'

The cup jumped through the presents, landing with a clang in front of her. Lotta glanced over her shoulder and lowered her voice.

'What are you doing here?'

'I could ask you the same question.' The cup stared up at her with ruby eyes. Lotta had borrowed the golden cup from Viking Chief Awfulrick to help her win a poetry contest. 'You told Awfulrick you were going to bring me back to Midgard over a month ago. But I'm still here!'

'I'm sorry,' Lotta snapped. 'I've been a bit busy saving the Nine Worlds. I haven't made it back to Midgard yet.'

The cup spun on the table, its squeaky voice cutting through the music. Lotta made a grab for it, but missed. 'I like being back in Asgard. I think Frigg missed me.'

Lotta peered over her shoulder, searching the crowd for the Goddess of Family – the original owner of the cup. Frigg was deep in conversation with a short woman whose long, dark plaits nearly reached her waist. Lotta flinched in shock and, without thinking, dived under the table. The cup jumped down to join her.

'What are you doing?'

'That's Glinting-Fire,' Lotta mumbled. Her knuckles cracked as she clenched her hands into fists, barely containing her anger. 'Freyja only invited her so it wouldn't

look suspicious. I can't let her see me.'

Glinting-Fire had tricked her way into her new position as Leader of the Valkyries and had tried to get rid of Lotta by destroying her Valkyrie shield, worried that Lotta would try to stop her evil plans for Valkyrie 'progress'. It hadn't worked.

'Good thinking.' The cup nodded. 'I'm sure no one will wonder why you're hiding under a table.'

'She doesn't know I'm back in Asgard,' Lotta hissed, peering out from between the table legs. Lotta had been careful to keep herself hidden from Glinting-Fire and the other Valkyries. Loki might have seen her transformation in Helheim, but there was no reason for Glinting-Fire to know that her plans had failed. Not yet anyway. 'Glinting-Fire would be furious if she knew Whetstone was here,' Lotta added with a smirk. 'She hates living humans. We found a report in the library about how she once got stranded on Midgard and had to disguise herself as a washerwoman. She'd scrubbed a whole village's socks before she got picked up.'

A pair of boots stopped next to the table and a smiling face appeared, looking down curiously at Lotta. 'Did you slip?' Freyr asked, offering her a hand.

'Er, I, no, I just –' Lotta stumbled as she climbed out, her face hot with embarrassment.

'Smooth,' the cup muttered.

The God of Summer regarded her carefully, his golden eyes standing out clearly against his thick lashes. Lotta forced a smile. With a brief bow, the man returned to the dancers.

Lotta released a breath she didn't realize she'd been

holding. 'This is too dangerous,' she muttered. 'Someone is going to start asking questions.'

'Questions like: Where is Odin?' the cup said loudly, bouncing up on to her shoulder. 'And: Why hasn't he come back to Asgard?'

'I suppose.' Lotta snatched at the cup.

'I made up a poem about that – would you like to hear it?'

'No!'

The cup coughed.

Why has Odin left Asgard?
Do you think he will send us a postcard?

Frigg peered over Glinting-Fire's shoulder. 'What is that girl doing with my cup?'

Glinting-Fire started to turn.

Panicking, Lotta threw the cup into the air. It landed with a smash in the middle of the dance floor, nearly braining Tyr, God of Justice. Eir, the Goddess of Healing, spun out of the way with quite an impressive pirouette. A stunned silence fell.

'DANCE BATTLE!' one of the musicians shouted.

All the Gods and Goddesses cheered. The musicians started playing again as the Gods stampeded towards the floor, all trying to outdo each other with their impressive moves.

In the group of musicians, Lotta caught Whetstone's eye. He winked. Lotta gave him a relieved thumbs-up, thankful that he had her back, before heading into the safety of the kitchens.

'Good idea,' the flute player wheezed to Whetstone. 'We don't get paid if they stop dancing.'

Whetstone nodded, his fingers slipping on the smooth frame of the harp. This party was unlike anything he had experienced in Midgard. Compared to the large, sweaty men and women throwing ale around that he was used to, this party was the height of sophistication. He gawked as Freyr moonwalked across the floor to collect a bowl of strawberries.

'You're getting the hang of it now,' the harpist next to Whetstone said. 'Just keep a steady rhythm and try not to break any more of the strings.'

Whetstone nodded, trying to focus on the music, his tongue sticking out of the corner of his mouth in concentration.

In his experience, harp strings were always trouble.

He had already managed to win one of the three cursed harp strings he'd been quested to find, but things hadn't gone smoothly and Whetstone had been forced to leave his father behind in Helheim. Now, for safekeeping, Whetstone wore the harp string like a necklace. A small charm in the shape of a fish hung from it, all that was left of the beads his father had used to disguise it.

Next to him, the harpist's fingers flew across the strings, picking out an intricate melody, which was immediately drowned out by the tone-deaf singing from the Gods.

Whetstone grinned as Glinting-Fire was dragged on to the dance floor. She was *not* a natural mover.

Trying to keep time with his harp, Whetstone wondered what he and Lotta were going to do. They couldn't stay in Asgard forever. In Odin's absence, Glinting-Fire had filled the chaotic world of the Gods with patrols, rules and organization. Surprisingly, no one had tried to stop her, regarding her efforts as an amusing personality quirk rather than what it actually was – a sinister attempt to seize control. There was no sign of Odin coming back, and wherever Loki was, Whetstone was sure he was up to no good. They had to find the next harp string before Loki got his hands on it.

Loki knew that Frigg's magic cup had given Whetstone a riddle to help him find the harp strings and his missing parents. That was why Loki was so determined to hunt Whetstone down. The second part of the riddle ran through Whetstone's mind in time to the music.

The other you will find, bound by a glittering chain.
She is kept for her tears, they fall as golden rain.

That half of the riddle was more useless than the first. At least the first half had been a clue about where to start looking for his father. But *golden tears* and *a glittering chain*? That could be anywhere. Whetstone winced as the harp string caught a paper cut on his finger. He thought of all the books and maps he had fruitlessly pored over in Freyja's library, searching for a helpful sentence like: *Here can be found a woman who cries golden tears* – but nothing. Maybe he would never find her?

'. . . cries golden tears, I heard,' Thor, God of Thunder, said loudly, wiping his red beard with the back of his hand.

Whetstone nearly fell over in shock.

'That would be a thing to have – never-ending treasure. Every time she cries, you get richer.'

'Who told you about it?' asked Tyr, shouting over the music.

Whetstone tried to shuffle sideways to hear better. A barrel-chested musician blew into a long battle horn, drowning out Thor's words with a sound like a cow mooing. Whetstone glared at him.

'Do you think that's what Odin is up to?' Tyr bellowed over the noise. 'Trying to get her out of Castle Utgard?'

Whetstone wobbled. The harpist gave him a concerned look. Whetstone had seen Castle Utgard on a map of Jotunheim: Land of the Giants. That must be where his mother was. A grin broke out across Whetstone's face. He looked happily at Freyja, no longer resenting the feathery hat or the stupid trousers. He had just found out where his mother was, and it had been SO easy! She quirked her eyebrows in return.

Thor shrugged. 'Maybe. I wouldn't mind taking a look for myself, though.' He hefted his hammer meaningfully.

'Rather you than me.' Tyr's mouth screwed up in distaste. 'Isn't Castle Utgard the one that human lad tried to break into? The Giants weren't too happy, I heard.'

Thor leaned closer. 'Definitely not happy. First they

20

grabbed his—'

The battle horn blasted in his ear again. Whetstone winced, his attention focused on Thor as he tried to lip-read the God's words.

'. . . then turned him into sausages.' Thor straightened up. 'Poor thing, didn't he know that only real Heroes like us stand a chance against Skrymir and his Giants?'

Whetstone gulped.

Maybe it wouldn't be *so* easy after all. Whetstone had heard stories about Skrymir, the biggest, baddest and most brutal of all the Frost Giants. Skrymir must live at Castle Utgard. Whetstone bit his lip, wondering how they would get past him. Lotta would probably have a plan – although, like her magic powers, her plans tended to backfire. Like the time she had tried to spy on the Valkyrie Training School and ended up stranded on the roof of Valhalla for three days.

Freyr shoulder-shimmied up to Thor and Tyr. In the silence between mooing noises, he shouted, 'Not dancing, Thor? I bet you've got some moves.'

Tyr finished his drink. 'Forget dancing – what we need is a good boast battle. Who wants to go first?'

Thor chuckled. 'Not me. I've not got the brains for the wordy stuff. The person you need is Loki.'

Whetstone shuddered. The battle horn nearly blasted all the feathers off his hat.

Carefully Lotta stepped out of the kitchens. In her arms she carried an enormous silver plate with a giant cake, modelled to look like Freyja, balancing on top of it. Spotting the cake,

Freyr whooped and danced away through the crowd, clearing a path for Lotta to a nearby table.

Freyja stood in the centre of the room, accepting everyone's birthday congratulations. The musicians struck up a new tune as the Gods sang, '*Happy birthday to you . . .*'

The harp string round Whetstone's neck rang out, high and clear over the rest of the instruments. Its special power was to warn when danger was near. Whetstone's blood froze in his veins, his chest felt tight. He gripped the harp string, trying to muffle the sound.

'*Happy birthday to you . . .*'

Whetstone's eyes raked the crowd. Something *very* bad was about to happen.

'*Happy birthday, dear Freyja . . .*'

'Yeah, Loki's who you're after.' Tyr chuckled. 'Where is that slippery Fire Giant? He's never around when you want him!'

'*Happy birthday to* you*!*'

Freyja picked up a knife to make the first slice. 'I'd like to thank you all for coming—'

With a flash of green light, the door to Freyja's Great Hall was blasted into toothpicks. Gods and Goddesses dived out of the way as the air filled with dust and curling green smoke. The battle horn shot across the room. Freyja's birthday cake exploded, coating Lotta in icing and crumbs. Whetstone hit the ground, knocked sideways by the flute player. He peeked out, his heart hammering.

It couldn't be . . .

Amid the coughing and spluttering, all eyes were fixed on the doorway. A tall, cloaked figure stepped inside. 'I'm sorry for not telling you I was coming, Freyja. My invitation must've got lost.'

At the sound of the figure's voice, Whetstone tried to sink into the floor. A cake-smeared Lotta stared open-mouthed as the smoke cleared to reveal a handsome man with collar-length blond hair. Scars twisted his smile into something sinister.

Loki.

Chapter Two

Boast Battle!

Freyja got to her feet, her beautiful gown covered in wooden splinters and splodges of cake. 'What are *you* doing here?'

Loki brushed some dust off his shoulder, his eyes scanning the icing-splattered crowd. Whetstone saw Lotta slide behind a couple of shocked-looking Goddesses to avoid his gaze. 'If I'd known it was your birthday, I'd have brought you a present. How old are you now, Freyja?'

The Goddess of Love and Sorcery sucked in a breath.

Her brother tutted, and wiped a smear of icing off his cheek. 'You had to ask.'

Loki smiled.

Thor pushed half a door off himself and stood up. 'Loki! We were just talking about you. You always know how to make an entrance!'

Loki ignored him, his eyes fixed on Freyja.

A grey figure appeared behind the Trickster. Vali leaned casually against the doorframe. His skin and clothes made of stone, a long crack running down one side of his face. Loki had turned his son into a Troll as a punishment for disobeying him months ago. A hard lump settled in Whetstone's stomach. Vali had helped him and Lotta escape Helheim, before being stranded there himself. But whose side was he on now? Loki must've brought Vali back to Asgard for a reason.

Other Gods and Goddesses started getting back to their feet, muttering about their cake-stained party clothes. A few of the younger Gods were grinning. Loki was always fun to have around – as long as you weren't his target.

Whetstone tried to hide his face as the musicians untangled themselves and got up, their feathery hats now in a big knot. Fear trickled down his spine.

'Where are you hiding them, Freyja?' Loki asked in a low voice.

Freyja tossed her gold-threaded twists. 'I don't know what you mean, Loki.'

Thor strode forward, oblivious to the tension. 'This is the man we need.' He wrapped his arm around Loki's shoulders, nearly knocking the Trickster out with his hammer.

Loki's dark eyes remained fixed on Freyja as Thor pulled him into the Great Hall. 'Good to see you've all missed me,' he said drily.

Freyja snorted. Her brother glanced from Freyja to Loki and back again. He whistled under his breath and, handing the stunned Lotta a large tray, started loading it up with anything easily breakable. Lotta soon vanished behind a tower of birthday presents.

Thor laughed, clapping Loki on the shoulder. 'We've had

the feasting and the dancing, now this party could do with a good boast battle. What do you say?'

Loki lifted an eyebrow. 'Gladly.' He turned in a slow circle, eyeing the crowd. 'I choose my opponent to be –' he tapped his scarred lip as people tried to avoid catching his eye. He stopped, facing Freyja – 'the birthday girl.'

'Ooooh,' the harpist next to Whetstone muttered. 'This should be good.'

With a burst of red light, the cake and splinters vanished from Freyja's clothes and hair, returning her to her normal pristine appearance. In a swirl of red and gold, she positioned herself in the centre of the Great Hall and gestured for Loki to join her.

The crowd shuffled out of the way to make space, birthday cake ground under many feet. Whetstone found himself pushed forward with the rest of the musicians. He ducked behind the flute player. Someone whooped – Loki's boast battles were always entertaining.

Tyr, the God of Justice, stepped between Freyja and Loki. 'The rules are: One – each competitor must improvise a boast about themselves or an insult about their competitor. Two – all boasts must rhyme. Three – audience reaction decides the winner. Freyja to go first.' Tyr stepped back again.

Low and intense notes filled the air as around Whetstone the musicians picked out a simple bassline to accompany the boasts. Thankfully, this drowned out the steady thrumming from the cursed harp string. Despite his fear of being caught,

26

Whetstone felt a thrill of excitement. He had watched boast battles between Vikings back on Midgard, but never anything where both competitors had magical powers and a serious grudge.

'Go on, Freyja!' Freyr called, his golden eyes gleaming. 'You can do this!' Beside him, Lotta's tray wobbled, sending cat ornaments sliding about.

The Goddess of Love and Sorcery looked Loki up and down with a sneer on her face. She raised her arms and turned to the crowd.

> *Listen well, you all know my name;*
> *I'm the Goddess who came from Vanaheim.*
> *I came to Asgard after the war;*
> *Part of the peace deal, that's what I'm for.*
> *Unlike you all, I've got powers and magic,*
> *And I look so good that I stop traffic!*

The crowd whooped. Even Whetstone grinned.

Loki smirked and replied:

> *Your magic is nothing, just cat hair and crumbs.*
> *You can't beat me, but don't be glum.*

Freyja crossed her arms as he went on.

> *You stand for love? Don't be tragic;*
> *You're not the only one who can do magic.*

Loki threw a fistful of green sparks into the air; they hung there glittering like emerald snowflakes. Whetstone reached out to touch one; it fizzled against his fingertip. The crowd cheered.

Freyja tossed her dark hair.

> *Loki – you're a mess.*
> *In distress.*
> *Why try to beat me when you know I'm the best?*

With a wave, she covered the walls with rubies. Loki curled his lip. Gods and Goddesses gasped. Freyja continued:

> *I'm here with my brother – I'm clever and strong.*
> *You are no one, and you're just plain wrong.*
> *Go back to Muspell, you'll find it easy;*
> *All you have to do is climb down the tree.*

The crowd howled in delight as Freyja and Loki stalked in circles, glaring at each other.

Loki held up his hands; the green sparks dropped to the floor.

> *Let's stop this game.*
> *Explain,*
> *Why do you hurt me – I'll just cause you pain?*
> *What has Asgard ever done for you?*
> *You want to protect them, but that's not up to you.*
> *Odin has gone and you're standing alone;*
> *You're going to lose, so just go home,*

Or join my side – I've got magic and fire.
The Nine Worlds are changing – I can raise you higher.

Freyja sucked her lip. Loki continued in a lower tone:

Give me the boy. He's nothing to you,
And if you get caught, there's nothing they won't do.

Loki gestured to the Gods eagerly watching the exchange. A chill ran up Whetstone's spine. The faces around him no longer looked pleasant but took on menacing expressions. Whetstone was sharply reminded that he and Lotta were fugitives here with barely any allies, alone and hunted by a powerful enemy . . .

He glanced around for the trainee Valkyrie, but she had vanished into the crowd.

Loki continued:

Play by their rules and you'll get burned.
Outsiders forever – it's time you learned
Your place.
You're a disgrace.
And you've got cake all over your face!

The crowd roared.

'Loki wins!' Thor cheered. He thumped the Trickster on the back, making him stumble. 'I didn't understand a word of it, but you got her!'

The ground started to tremble as Freyja clenched her fists, rubies tumbling from the walls of her elegant hall. 'Party's over. Everyone out.'

'Come on, Freyja. Don't be a bad loser.' Freyr approached his sister. 'It was just fun.'

Freyja stamped her foot. 'I said *out*!'

Grumbling and muttering, the Gods and Goddesses started towards the shattered doors. Loki smirked at their disappointed faces but made no move to follow them.

'Nice one, Loki,' a man with a golden beard muttered as he headed out. Vali stood like a stone against the tide of party guests. Around Whetstone the musicians started packing away their instruments. There was a heated discussion about who was going to ask Freyja for their payment.

As the crowd thinned, Whetstone finally spotted Lotta. She was pinned to the floor next to the tray of presents by Freyja's big fluffy cat, Mr Tiddles. The cat sat on her lap, his claws digging into her legs as he purred loudly. Lotta held her nose, her cheeks puffed out with the effort of not sneezing.

Whetstone ducked away from the musicians and fought his way across the room to try and remove Mr Tiddles before it was too late. Lotta was highly allergic to cats and, as an unfortunate side effect, every time she sneezed her new magic powers backfired. Loki might not have noticed them so far, but even he couldn't fail to miss a fountain of feathers or something.

'Ah – Ah –!' Lotta's face screwed up; her eyes closed.

Keeping one eye on Loki, who was busy arguing with

Freyja, Whetstone skidded under a table to try and reach the unfortunate Valkyrie. The harp string around his neck thrummed loudly.

Loki's head snapped round, following the sound. 'You!' he snarled. Freyja snatched at his sleeve, pulling him off balance as he tried to shove her out of the way. Together they tumbled into a group of party goers. 'Vali, stop him!'

Vali took a step forward but was caught in the crush by the doorway as half of Freyja's guests stopped to see what all the fuss was about, and the other half were still trying to leave.

'Ah – AH –!'

Whetstone yanked Mr Tiddles away from Lotta, leaving long rips in her silky clothes.

'ACHOO!' Purple flames shot out of Lotta's nose and mouth, blasting halfway across the room. Shrieking filled the air from the Gods and Goddesses as they were almost set alight. The cat leaped out of Whetstone's arms, landing halfway up one of Freyja's favourite tapestries.

Freyja stepped forward, waving her arms through clouds of purple smoke. 'Get out or I'll do it again –' she coughed – 'I'll set the lot of you on fire!'

Gods and Goddesses stampeded towards the doors, dragging a protesting Vali out with them.

Whetstone yanked Lotta to her feet and hustled her into the kitchens. Loki had seen Lotta's powers changing in Helheim – there was no way he would believe that was Freyja.

'I'm sorry.' Lotta wiped her nose. 'You know I can't help it.'

A shadow with plaits sticking out from either side of its

31

helmet loomed through the kitchen door. The boy and girl recoiled.

'It's Glinting-Fire!' Lotta hissed. She reached behind her, fingers scrabbling on the table for a weapon. Her hand closed around something. 'We have to get out, now!' She swung her arm forward, brandishing a – ladle?

'Nice spoon.' Whetstone pushed open the window shutters and started to climb through. 'Argh!' With a flash of green light, Whetstone was dragged back into the room and hoisted high into the air by one foot. The thrumming harp string smacked into his face, the fish charm whacking him in the eye.

'Going somewhere, Whetstone?' Loki called from the Great Hall.

Lotta grabbed Whetstone, trying to pull him back down. His feathery hat poking her in the face. 'Good thing we made a plan for this.' She sniffed, her nose wrinkling.

'We did?'

'Yes! Plan seventeen is go. ACHOO!'

Whetstone dropped heavily to the ground, knocked free by Lotta's sneeze. 'Which one was plan seventeen?' he asked, wiping his face.

Glinting-Fire stepped into the room. 'Brings-A-Lot-Of-Scrapes-And-Grazes, where are you?' The tattooed lines on her face scrunched up in a snarl.

'Just leaving,' Lotta replied, perched on the windowsill. She held up the cursed harp string, making Whetstone fumble at his neck. As she dropped out of the windowsill and into the darkness, Lotta called back, 'Remember, plan seveeeeeenteeeeeen!'

32

Whetstone scrambled to his feet, desperate to follow Lotta out of the kitchen and get back his harp string. 'Come near me, and I'll touch you with my *living human hands*!' He waggled his fingers at Glinting-Fire, remembering her revulsion of living humans.

The short Valkyrie gagged. Loki appeared behind Glinting-Fire, the smirk disappearing from his face as he realized Whetstone wasn't trapped by his magic. 'How did you—?'

With a wave, Whetstone jumped through the window and out into the rutted alley below. Crushing what was left of his feathery hat beneath his boots, he scuttled away into the night.

'Whetstone, you can't escape!' Loki bellowed. 'I have friends everywhere!'

Whetstone picked up speed. Running away was something he had always been good at.

It was just a shame it wasn't very Hero-like.

Chapter Three

The Place Where Heroes Go

Whetstone slowed, a stitch growing in his side. 'Lotta?' he hissed. 'Where are you?' Occasional clay lamps lit the endless, twisting lanes of Asgard, but nothing looked familiar in the dark. He could be running in a big circle, and it would be just his luck to bump into Loki while searching for Lotta.

Footsteps echoed off the nearby buildings, making it sound like a whole platoon of people were marching towards him. Heart thumping, Whetstone ducked into the shadows as a group of Gods and Goddesses appeared, glowing gently in the darkness.

'I can't believe Freyja threw us out like that.'

'The purple fire was *well harsh*.'

'Yeah, bruv.'

'Just cos she's from Vanaheim, thinks she's too posh for us.'

'Loki was good though.'

'Yeah, bruv.'

'Did you hear Thor talking about the Giants?'

'Golden tears? 'Snot worth it – Giants can be *nasty*.'

'Yeah, bruv.'

'Shut *up*, Narvi.'

Whetstone pressed his shoulder blades into the doorframe behind him, keeping his head low as they passed. His elbows tight in at his sides. Thor must've told everyone about the woman who cried golden tears. Whetstone sucked in a breath trying to calm his racing heartbeat. Loki hadn't heard the riddle, so he didn't know why the woman was so important. But there was no time to waste waiting for him to figure it out. Besides, the last thing Whetstone needed was for *another* God to get involved and rescue her first. Whetstone had to find Lotta and get to his mum – *quick*.

Whetstone peered out into the now-empty street. Just one problem: he had no idea where Lotta, or even where *he*, was. He would have to find somewhere to wait until daybreak, or until he remembered what plan seventeen was.

Whetstone sighed. Lotta had made So. Many. Plans. Covering anything and everything that might happen to them, often with diagrams and flowcharts. Unfortunately, Whetstone had stopped listening after about plan five. Lotta had even taken his harp string – he felt oddly naked without it – but clearly this was part of the infamous plan seventeen.

Whetstone trailed his fingers along a rough wooden fence. A gap appeared where some planks had come away.

He peered around – this seemed as good a place as any to hide. The boy squeezed through the gap, his baggy breeches catching on splintery wood. He hitched them up, grumbling.

Flashes of green magic lit up the distant sky, followed by a rolling boom and some screams. Whetstone flinched, his shoulders up around his ears. Loki must be ripping apart Asgard searching for him. But at least he was looking in the wrong place. For now.

Sliding down the fence, Whetstone stretched out his legs and tipped his head back. He closed his eyes, trying to think. He couldn't afford to make any more mistakes. This time he was going to do things right.

Thor had said his mum was being held prisoner in Castle Utgard by the Frost Giants. If there was one thing Thor knew a lot about, it was the Frost Giants. He was always beating them up with his magic hammer. Whetstone rubbed his face, the fear that had propelled him this far draining away, leaving tiredness behind. Thor had also said that the last human to enter Castle Utgard had been turned into sausages.

Whetstone gulped. He did not fancy becoming a Giant's breakfast. His thoughts began to spin. Only Gods and Heroes had even a chance of beating the Giants. Technically he was a Hero – Odin had said so – but the boy doubted his particular type of sneaky Heroism was going to get him very far with the Frost Giants. They might be big and clumsy, but they also had a slow sort of cunning, which was hard to fool for long.

A shard of guilt twisted in Whetstone's chest. Of course, if he'd been any good at being a Hero in the first place, he wouldn't have left his dad behind.

Whetstone's eyes drifted across the moonlit skyline. A huge building thatched with spears poked up higher than the rest. Words to an old song drifted through his memory.

> *Valhalla! Valhalla!*
> *The place where Heroes go.*
> *Valhalla! Valhalla!*
> *When they're slain by their foe.*

An idea started to form. Maybe he could learn from the Heroes of Valhalla? They were the best of the best of the best. The greatest fighters, the bravest warriors, and the ultimate in what Midgard had to offer. Whetstone felt his heart speed up. If he was more like them, he might be able to rescue his mum without messing it up. He could become someone who could deal with Giants and monsters without running away or hiding. Someone fearless, tough, and with witty quips ready for every occasion.

In other words: a proper Hero.

❄

Lotta shrank into the shadows as another troop of Valkyries marched past. She wrinkled her nose. Valkyries shouldn't be all wooden and matchy-matchy like that. It felt wrong. The Valkyrie Leader had wasted no time in sending out patrols to search for them.

Thanks to Loki, Glinting-Fire now knew she and Whetstone were somewhere in Asgard and that her plans to get rid of Lotta had failed. Lotta wiggled her shoulders. They'd been strangely lucky that Glinting-Fire hadn't figured it out before, really.

Lotta glared as the shiny armoured Valkyries poked into corners and peered into doorways. Her heart ached as she recognized Fetid and Dire from her class in the Valkyrie Training School. She'd fix everything and Asgard would be back to normal soon, she silently promised them.

Previously, under Scold, the Valkyries had been a patchwork of women and girls. It hadn't mattered where you were from or what skills you had, as long as you worked hard to serve Odin by bringing fallen warriors back to Valhalla to build his army ready for Ragnarok, the battle at the end of the world.

There were three classes of Valkyrie. Students moved up from Class Three to Class Two and finally on to Class One as their skills in six key areas improved. Lotta hadn't been the greatest trainee – OK, she was probably the worst trainee – but even she had been making improvements.

Valkyrie Training School Report

Name: Brings-A-Lot-Of-Scrapes-And-Grazes (Lotta)

Class:	**Third**	
Skill	**Current Score**	**Previous Scores**
Fighting:	0%	(40%) (35%)
Horse Riding:	0%	(42%) (30%)
Epic Poetry:	0%	(30%) (28%)
Transforming into Swans:	0%	(51%) (38%)
Serving Mead in Valhalla:	0%	(57%) (53%)
Collecting Fallen Warriors:	0%	(59.9%) (0%)
Overall Hero Score:	0%	(47%) (31%)

Signed: *Glinting-Fire*, New Leader of the Valkyries

❀

An individual Valkyrie's score was shown on her circular shield. The shields were split into six sections, each section glowing according to how high their score was. Well, that was how it used to work. Now all the Valkyrie shields, other than Lotta's, had been encased in magical green ice by Loki, turning the Valkyries into enchanted zombies who did everything Glinting-Fire told them to. Despite all her reading and research, Lotta hadn't yet found a way of breaking Loki's spell, and even Freyja had been unable to help as her Goddess magic differed from Loki's Giant magic.

Following a signal, the Valkyrie troop finished their search and marched away, their boots hitting the ground in unison.

Lotta tugged the hair wrap off her head and scratched at her black curls. As terrified as she was of Loki or Glinting-Fire catching them, it felt good to be actually *doing* something. She was tired of all the hiding and sneaking around. It wasn't exactly the Valkyrie way. The Valkyrie way being more *charging at the enemy while screaming and trying to chop their knees off.* With a sigh, Lotta stepped out of the shadows.

A dark shape loomed over her. 'Where are *you* going?'

Lotta fumbled for the object in her belt. Heart hammering, she swung it out in front of her like a sword.

'Planning on spooning me to death?'

Lotta looked along the length of the ladle and into a stony grey face. Before Loki had turned him into a Troll, Vali had been a tall, good-looking boy with a fascination for sharp objects.

'It's not my fault,' Lotta explained, not lowering the ladle. There was no telling whose side Vali was on – this minute, anyway. 'They wouldn't let me carry my sword. Said it didn't go with the disguise.'

Vali barked a laugh, his voice sounding rough. 'By "they",
you mean Freyja?' Lotta tried not to twitch. 'It's not exactly
a secret,' Vali continued. 'We all saw her rescue you from
Helheim.' Vali shoved his hand through his dark hair. Lotta's
skin prickled with shame: she and Whetstone had intended to
return to Helheim to rescue Vali; they just hadn't got around
to it.

Lotta lowered the ladle a fraction. 'How did you convince
Loki to bring you back to Asgard? And how do you move so
quietly!'

Vali smiled, his teeth gleaming like pebbles. 'Father seems
to think I might be useful.'

Sourness bubbled in Lotta's stomach. 'You're helping him
again, after everything he did?'

Vali shrugged. 'If I was helping him, I would've told him
when I first spotted you at the party. You've still got cake in
your hair, by the way.'

Lotta scrubbed at her black curls.

'And if you're trying to hide, you really shouldn't be lurking
outside our house.'

'I'm nowhere near your house. It's over by –' Lotta wheeled
around in a circle – 'oh.' Loki's low, dark house sat at the end
of the passageway. Lotta grimaced. 'I must've got confused in
the dark.'

A cascade of sparks lit up the night sky, turning the silver
snakes on Loki's front door green. Instinctively Lotta raised
the ladle.

'Father isn't happy you got away from Freyja's.' Vali twisted a short knife between his fingers, the magical green light reflecting off his grey skin. 'He's not going to let you go again. He and Glinting-Fire will lock Asgard down and squeeze you and Whetstone out street by street, house by house if they have to. If you think things have been bad so far, you have no idea what's coming.'

A boom echoed down the twisting street, followed by angry shrieks. Lotta ducked, coughing as dust filled the air. Vali brushed himself down. 'Looks like Father thought you might be hiding with Eir. I hope she's got somewhere else she can sleep tonight.'

The ladle wobbled in Lotta's hand. 'Why come back then? If things are going to be so bad here, why not stay in Helheim?' Lotta tossed her head. 'Or is it because you're Loki's golden boy again and you'll be fine whatever he's planning?'

Fingers of green smoke twisted down the narrow street behind Vali, brushing against buildings and creeping up to shuttered windows. Lotta backed away, leaving Vali standing ankle-deep in the mist.

'I'm not an idiot – I did what I had to do to get out of Helheim. From Asgard I can use the Bifrost Bridge to reach Midgard.' Vali tucked the knife back into his belt. 'I'd do the same if I were you. Now. This time tomorrow, no one will be getting in or out.'

A cold tremor ran down Lotta's spine.

Vali's face creased into a smile, the long crack that ran down the side of his face making him look more like his father than ever. 'Look after yourself, Lotta. Maybe I'll see you again when the worlds open.' Turning, Vali disappeared into the swirling mists.

Sprinting away from the green fog, Lotta stuck her hand into her pocket to feel for the harp string. It vibrated quietly against her sweaty palm. She hoped that meant Loki hadn't found Whetstone yet. She had to get the harp string into its hiding place, then find Whetstone. Vali was right – they had to get out of Asgard as soon as possible.

Lotta curled the harp string around her fingers. She felt bad about taking it from Whetstone, but he would understand – it was part of the plan, after all.

Silken tunic whispering, Lotta peered around the next corner, her ears pricked for more Valkyrie footsteps. Her destination lay just ahead. The place where she planned to hide the harp string. The safest place in Asgard.

The place where Heroes go.

As the rising sun sent pink streaks across the bronze sky, the heavy door to the enormous hall creaked open. The gluey scent of porridge filled the air, mixed with old socks, spilt drinks and bodily injury. Valhalla was the place every Viking dreamed of going after death. But only the bravest Heroes and the greatest warriors were selected. Whetstone grinned. These were just the people he wanted to meet.

The door swung shut behind him, plunging him into stuffy darkness. Inside, the walls stretched for miles and the ceiling was lost in the gloom. Tables the size of boats filled the space, each one overflowing with scar-covered people. Candles hung from the distant ceiling, making the hall feel like a giant, badly lit cave. Whetstone swallowed his nerves and shuffled forward; he had never been inside Valhalla before.

A large sign was nailed to the wall by the doorway.

NO Weapons in Valhalla.

A pile of swords and axes lay abandoned beneath it.

The boy pushed back his shoulders and resisted the urge to pull his hood up over his head. 'Odin said I was a Hero – I have as much right to be here as anyone else,' he muttered, trying not to look at any of the more brutal injuries. In the distance Valkyries dropped off cauldrons of porridge at the different tables. Whetstone's stomach rumbled.

The Heroes and warriors of Valhalla all looked as they had in life, but now a blue glow surrounded them, showing that they were there through Odin's magic. Despite having fought each other on Midgard, there were no enemies here. Warriors from rival villages sat together peacefully, until it was time to go out on to the field beside the Great Hall and practise their biting, kicking, gouging and sword fighting, that is. Any injuries were magically healed, and everyone always had great fun.

Whetstone's eyes landed on a scrap of paper lying on the nearest table. He picked it up.

VALHALLA REIGNING CHAMPIONS

Axe-throwing: Fenna the Thrifty (eighty-seven paces. Backwards).

Barrel-lifting: Engelbert the Eagle Botherer (disqualified for dropping the barrel).

Horse-wrestling: Ottar the One-Armed.

Shin-kicking: ~~Frodi the Flint Toed~~ Jorunn the Iron-Shinned.

Single combat: Stinky Stein (weapon of choice: body odour).

NO-rules wrestling (no weapons): Alvar the Biter.

NO-rules wrestling (weapons): Alvar the Battler (no relation to Alvar the Biter).

Falconry: Eric the Elegant, with Doris the Falcon.

'Thinking of competing, are yeh?' said a voice by his ear.

Whetstone tried not to react. 'What is it? Some sort of contest?' He turned to look at the owner of the voice. The man was short and bald with longish arms and swirling tattoos picked out against his suntanned skin.

The man tapped the paper. 'Those are the best of Valhalla. The strongest, the bravest, the most Heroic.'

Whetstone felt his insides tingle. This paper contained a list of the greatest warriors in Valhalla, the perfect people to teach him how to be a Hero.

The man grinned, showing blue-stained teeth. 'Which contest were you thinking of?'

'Oh, I don't think I'm ready for –' Whetstone began.

The man crossed his arms. 'Are you turning down a challenge?'

'No, I just meant –' Whetstone gabbled. 'I'm new – I wouldn't want to step on anyone's toes.'

'Toe-crushing is on Wednesdays,' said a passing woman with long red braids.

'What sort of Hero turns down a challenge?' The man's eyes narrowed. 'Are you sure you're in the right place? You *are* dressed like a musician . . .'

'No, no! I *am* a Hero, and I'll prove it.' Whetstone stabbed a finger randomly down on the page. 'I'll do that one.' He hoped he hadn't picked horse-wrestling, which sounded ridiculous. He could probably manage axe-throwing or falconry, as long as the falcons weren't too heavy. The man glanced at the paper and raised an eyebrow. Whetstone raised one in return.

The man grinned again, then yelled into the gloom, 'Stinky Stein! I've got a challenger for you!' The man slapped Whetstone on the back, knocking him forward so his legs whacked into the table.

A distant table of heavily built men erupted into cheers. A very hairy man dressed in equally hairy clothing wiped porridge from his mouth with the back of his hand and got to his feet.

'Stinky Stein, Stinky Stein, Stinky Stein!' his friends cheered, drumming on the table.

Whetstone frantically scrabbled for the paper – hopefully it *was* axe-throwing. He ran his finger down the page. 'Stinky Stein . . . *Single combat?*'

The bald man laughed. 'And here was me thinking you were a bit weaselly-looking. You must be brave, taking on Stinky Stein.' The man dropped his voice, pointing at a warrior sitting across the room. 'Aelfric tried it last week and he still hasn't recovered.' The man, Aelfric, raised his head. A large bowl sat on the table in front of him, clouds of steam wafting up, filling the air with the scent of herbs. 'The Valkyries say he should get his sense of smell back, eventually.'

Whetstone stared. 'Um –'

The bald man turned back to Whetstone. 'It could've been worse – you could've got me.'

'Who are you?'

The man flashed his stained teeth again. 'Alvar the Biter.'

47

Chapter Four

Rhett the Bone-Breaker

Deep in Valhalla's armoury, Whetstone hurriedly pulled on a chainmail shirt followed by a breastplate. Feeling like Lotta, he wrapped leather strips around his forearms for added protection. With a pang, Whetstone realized he hadn't thought about her or the harp string once since entering Valhalla. He hoped they were both all right. Lotta might be set on plan seventeen, whatever that was, but he had his own plans in action now.

Whetstone eyed the bench in front of him. Notched and heavy-looking weapons covered its surface. There were things he recognized and things he didn't. Long curved swords, spears that were taller than he was, and a nasty-looking pole with a hook on the end. The boy shuddered – if he was going to rescue his mum from the Land of the Giants and be a proper Hero, he was going to have to get used to fighting and using weapons.

Whetstone's hand passed over the blades – instead he picked up a silver-and-gold helmet. It was covered in fine carvings and the face guard had an impressive golden moustache. He turned it over in his hands – this was the type of thing a true warrior would wear!

The door opened behind him with a crash. Whetstone slammed the helmet on his head, trying to line up his eyes with the eyeholes. The helmet had clearly been made for someone with a larger skull.

'All ready?' Alvar demanded before dropping a long-handled axe into Whetstone's arms. 'Don't forget this.'

Whetstone gulped. His tongue suddenly felt too big for his mouth.

Alvar gave him a shove towards the door. 'Get out there and show them what you're made of!'

This did not help as, unfortunately, Whetstone knew exactly what he was made of. Squidgy bits and easily cut things. The axe nearly slipped through his trembling fingers.

Outside, a boiling green cloud filled half the bronze sky, the sun looking sickly behind it. The air felt thick and heavy. Outlines of shattered buildings poked up here and there along Asgard's skyline. Whetstone gulped; Loki had been busy. The boy forced his mind back to the task in front of him. His single-combat challenge had attracted quite a crowd, but thankfully no sign of the Trickster. Fallen Heroes and warriors chatted in small huddles, their eyes flicking to the green clouds, worried expressions on their faces.

In the centre of the field stood Stinky Stein and his cronies. Stinky Stein still wearing his thick furry clothes. Whetstone felt a trickle of sweat run down the back of his neck. No wonder they called him stinky if he never took that lot off.

49

Whetstone tramped across the field. Why couldn't he have started with the feasting, or the singing loud songs, rather than going straight for the fighting? He should have eased his way into being a Hero. Whetstone's mind swung from one idea to another: from the bone-numbing fear that he was about to be chopped into tiny pieces by someone with a terrible body-odour problem, to the confidence that maybe, somehow, this would all work out.

He came to a halt opposite Stinky Stein. 'He's not got a weapon,' Whetstone whispered to Alvar. Relief swept over him. That would definitely even things up a bit. Whetstone tried to stand up straight, hoping the golden moustache would give him a dignified look.

'Didn't you read the list of champions?' Alvar replied. 'His weapon of choice is body odour. I hope you're good at holding your breath.'

Stinky Stein grinned at him over a nose shaped like an onion.

A tall man dressed in black stepped between them. In a growly voice he announced, 'Weighing in at one hundred and forty-seven turnips, from the town of Sullen Dip, I give you the undefeated Single Combat Champion of Valhalla!' The crowd roared.

The fur-covered man stepped towards Whetstone. 'Stinky Stein!' Stein bellowed, raising his arms into the air. Whetstone was nearly knocked sideways by a rolling cloud of body odour. It was impossible to describe what it smelt like as his human nose just shut down. Whetstone thought there might be cheese in there somewhere . . . and root vegetable.

'Stinky Stein!' the warriors chanted back.

The man in black turned to Whetstone. 'Weighing in at, probably what? Fifteen turnips? I give you, the single combat challenger!'

Whetstone swallowed his fear and took a step forward. Everyone looked at him expectantly.

'You have to tell them your name,' Alvar hissed.

This was the moment: no more useless Whetstone from Drott. Now he could choose a Heroic new name. A new identity . . . Someone brave, confident, courageous and bold.

'I am Whetstone –' the boy squeaked.

'Wet the Stone?' muttered someone.

'Did he say, Vett the Toned?'

'No, Jet the Groan.'

'He said, Rhett the Bone!' called one of the warriors confidently.

'Rhett the Bone-what? I can't hear,' complained another.

'Give me a break,' Whetstone muttered, trying to shove his helmet out of his eyes.

'Bone-Breaker!' Alvar shouted.

'Rhett the Bone-Breaker?' the warriors repeated, sounding slightly unconvinced.

The man in black shrugged. 'Stinky Stein, Rhett the Bone-Breaker, the rules are simple. Fight until one of you gives in!' With the clang of a bell, the tall man bowed out of the way.

Whetstone hefted his axe. He had never fought anyone with an axe before. It looked pretty simple though: you just had to hit them with the sharp bit. 'I am Rhett the Bone-Breaker, and I am going to beat Stinky Stein, then rescue my mum from Castle Utgard,' Whetstone muttered. 'And I'm going to do it all without breathing through my nose.'

Stein rolled up his sleeves, his forearms the size of tree trunks. Around them the warriors started to stamp their feet. Stein and Whetstone circled each other. Whetstone waved the axe forward, half not wanting to hit his opponent with it. Stein grabbed the axe and yanked it out of Whetstone's hands. He tossed it away over his shoulder.

Whetstone grimaced. Now he had no weapon and no chance. He wondered if Rhett the Bone-Breaker was any good at running.

Stein caught hold of Whetstone's chainmail shirt, lifting the boy up so they were nose to nose. The smell was stronger the closer you got to Stein; Whetstone thought he could feel the wax running out of his ears.

Stein grinned, his teeth white against his dark beard. 'What I'm gonna do first is—'

But he never got to finish saying what he was going to do, as with a metallic thump, something struck the back of Stein's head. He dropped Whetstone before crashing forward like a felled tree, landing on top of the boy.

Whetstone gasped, trying to breathe and not breathe at the same time. A cross brown face topped by a helmet appeared over Stein's shoulder. Dark curls poked out around the edge.

'Lotta?' Whetstone panted.

The tall man waved his arms. 'This is against the rules! It's supposed to be single combat, but you're working as a team.'

'No, we're not,' Lotta replied hotly, her hands on her hips. 'And where does it say only two competitors at a time?'

The Heroes and warriors looked at each other in confusion.

'So, you're now going to fight –' the tall man pointed at Whetstone, who had managed to wiggle out from under Stinky Stein and was sniffing himself gingerly – 'him?'

Lotta nodded.

'Wait, *we're* fighting now?' Whetstone said, looking up.

'We need to get out of Asgard.' Lotta thrust the axe back into his arms. 'Why couldn't you stick to plan seventeen?'

'I could've sworn this was it.' Whetstone grinned.

Lotta glowered, then turned to the crowd. 'I am Dagmar the Destroyer!'

The crowd cheered. They didn't mind who did the fighting as long as someone did. A couple of Stein's friends dragged him off the battlefield.

Lotta pulled a *ladle* out of her belt. Whetstone looked at her in confusion. 'What's that?'

'I left my sword at Freyja's. Now just make it look good, and maybe we'll get out of here alive, *Rhett*.' Lotta swung her ladle; Whetstone managed to fend it off with the axe. 'Is that your new name? Should I start calling you that?'

'There was some confusion –' the ladle boinged off Whetstone's helmet – 'I didn't really get a chance to explain, *Dagmar*.'

Lotta narrowed her eyes.

'Anyway, why shouldn't I have a Heroic name? I am a Hero, after all.'

'And you thought you'd prove it by fighting Stinky?'

Whetstone swung the axe wildly. 'I got a bit caught up in the moment. I didn't want to disappoint anyone. Where's the harp string?'

'I hid it,' Lotta hissed, spinning around

54

for another attack. 'As per plan seventeen.'

'Oh, I forgot – perfect plan seventeen,' Whetstone grumped as he managed to parry with his axe.

'Yes, plan seventeen: I hide the harp string so Loki can't trick its location out of you, and you get the key to the gates so we can get out of Asgard. We don't have time for this *messing about*!'

The warriors *Ooohed* as Whetstone ducked under the ladle. 'Oh, *that* was plan seventeen. Why can't you just use your powers and fly us out?' Whetstone stumbled and the axe swung upward as he overbalanced, slicing towards Lotta's face. She threw out her arm to block the blow. The axe bounced off and, with a burst of feathers, Lotta vanished – in her place stood a large dog.

'Actually, I don't think I trust

you to fly us anywhere.' Whetstone smirked. 'This is new. Should I get you a flea collar?'

The dog sneezed and Lotta reappeared. The warriors gasped.

'I forfeit the fight,' Lotta yelled, chucking down her ladle. 'We need to go – now!'

The ladle burst into purple flames. Above them the green cloud swirled, as if disturbed by the magic.

'I, Rhett the Bone-Breaker, am the champion!' Whetstone cheered, waving his axe. 'I told you I was a Hero!'

'You're going to get all our bones broken if we don't get out of here!' Lotta grabbed his arm.

The Heroes and warriors started to mutter. Whetstone lowered his axe.

'Heroes don't cheat with magic!' Lotta spluttered.

'But I didn't do anything!'

'They don't know that! They'll think you're a wizard.'

Whetstone grimaced and threw down the axe, nearly slicing off one of his own toes. 'Run?'

Lotta nodded. Together they sprinted away from the confused-looking warriors, back through the narrow streets towards the heart of Asgard.

After a few minutes, Whetstone jogged to a halt. He tugged off the helmet and rested his hands on his knees to get his breath back. 'You have got to stop doing that.'

Lotta pulled him into the shadows. 'Doing what? Saving your life? You could say thank you.'

Tendrils of green mist slunk towards them.

'No –' he waved a hand up and down at her – '*that*. The flames and the feathers and the random dog.'

Lotta gritted her teeth as she eyed the approaching fog. 'It happens when I get stressed. They just sort of – pop out.'

Something bumped into Whetstone's ankles, making him yelp. His helmet clattered to the ground, nearly squishing a brown, furry cat, who stared up at Whetstone with a resentful expression.

Whetstone picked up the helmet. 'Is that – Mr Tiddles?'

'Looks like it, ACHOO!' Lotta grumpily brushed feathers off her clothes. 'What does he want?'

Content that he had their attention, the cat sat down and began washing his face with his paw.

Whetstone shrugged. 'Do you think Freyja wants to see us?'

'We can't go back to her Great Hall,' Lotta muttered, pinching her nose. 'It's the first place Loki and Glinting-Fire would look.'

'Or maybe it's the *best* place to go because they'll already have searched there?' Whetstone pondered. The cat stretched and sauntered away, its tail flicking around the corner for them to follow.

Still holding her nose, Lotta tipped her head in thought. 'Freyja *has* still got my sword and shield . . .' She peered around the corner after the cat. Freyja's Great Hall sat at the end of the lane, its red doors swinging crookedly as the cat slipped inside. No mist surrounded it. 'It does *look* quiet.'

Whetstone peered over her shoulder. 'So did Helheim.'

Lotta narrowed her eyes. Whetstone knew she was picturing her sword and shield – there was no way she would leave Asgard without them if she could help it.

'And since you didn't get the key, we *do* still need to find a way out of Asgard,' the girl muttered, her gaze fixed on the Great Hall. 'Freyja could help us . . .'

The boy gave her a poke. 'So, this isn't part of plan seventeen?'

Lotta growled at him over her shoulder.

Whetstone sighed and stuck the helmet back on his head. There was no arguing with the trainee Valkyrie when she was in this mood. 'Come on, let's go check it out.'

Chapter Five

Cloak of Many Feathers

Freyja's Great Hall had been a mess when Whetstone and Lotta left, doors smashed open by Loki and birthday cake everywhere. But that was nothing compared to the devastation in front of them now. Every stick of furniture shattered. Every cushion sliced open. In the centre of it all sat Freyja on a stool, delicately eating the last slice of birthday cake with a golden

fork. Mr Tiddles deftly picked his way through the chaos to Freyja's side.

Broken plates crunched under Lotta's sandals as she made her way across the room, pinching her nose to stop the sneezing.

'Do you think it's actually Freyja?' Whetstone muttered out of the corner of his mouth. 'It could be Loki shapeshifting again.'

'Loki has grown too arrogant to think he needs to disguise himself any more, especially not as me,' the woman answered, finishing her cake. 'He believes he beat me at the party, so he's playing other games now.'

Lotta caught Whetstone's eye and gulped.

Abruptly Freyja frisbeed the plate across the room. It smashed against the wall, making the cat hiss and Lotta and Whetstone flinch. 'Nice work, Mr T,' Freyja said to the cat at her feet. 'Now check they weren't followed.'

The cat stretched and sauntered back to the door, his tail flicking from side to side. Lotta squeezed her nose against the drifting cat hair.

'Why are you two still in Asgard?' Freyja licked icing off her fingers. 'You should be long gone.'

'How?' Lotta crossed her arms. 'Genius here didn't stick to plan seventeen.'

Whetstone scratched his neck. 'You can't expect me to do everything you say.'

Lotta snorted. 'Vali said we should use the Bifrost Bridge, but they'll be watching for us.'

'Wait, you spoke to Vali?' Whetstone spluttered. 'Did he say anything about my dad?'

Lotta ignored him; she focused on Freyja. 'You should come with us. Before Loki and Glinting-Fire come back for another go.'

Whetstone glanced at the wreckage around them. 'Yeah, I'm sorry about –' he gestured at the room. 'I guess this was the Valkyries?'

'They're all being mind-controlled,' Lotta spluttered. 'This isn't usual Valkyrie behaviour.' She squirmed as behind them a shelf collapsed, scattering cat ornaments over the floor. Avoiding everyone's gaze, Lotta started poking through the mess. 'I'll just find my sword and shield and then we'll go.'

Freyja's eyes narrowed. 'You'll need more than that to beat the Giants.'

Lotta looked up. 'But we're not –'

'How did you know –' Whetstone said at the same time.

'Thor told *everyone* that story about the woman who cried golden tears in Castle Utgard,' Freyja explained with a toss of her head.

'He didn't tell me,' Lotta muttered, yanking her breastplate out from under a pile of smashed dishes. 'The *plan* was to get Scold back from Alfheim.'

'Things change,' Whetstone muttered. 'You're obsessed with those plans, and they never go right.'

'That's because *you* don't listen!'

'I was doing fine on my own!'

Lotta looked up from tightening the straps of her breastplate over her billowy clothing. 'Yeah, so you weren't about to be rolled into a ball and kicked around Valhalla by Stinky Stein?'

Whetstone snorted; the Valkyrie now looked like a battle-ready pillowcase. 'At least I don't turn into dogs or ducks or Odin knows what every time I sneeze.'

'Hey! I'm *trying* to finish this quest! I even did special interrogation training with Freyja.' Lotta sniffed. 'Loki's not going to get the location of the harp string out of me!'

'No?' Whetstone scoffed. 'He's just got to waft some cat hair at you. We'll never be able to rescue my mum if you keep exploding every five minutes!'

'You know I can't help that! And what about you?' Lotta spluttered. 'I'm not sure I want to hang out with Rhett the Bone-Breaker – he looks like a right—'

'That's enough!' Freyja snapped. 'The Nine Worlds are in danger and you two are bickering like an old married couple!'

Lotta's eyes bulged. Whetstone's mouth opened and closed noiselessly.

Freyja gave a tight smile. 'Have you forgotten what is at stake?' With a wave of her hand, an image of a tree appeared, conjured out of red sparks. It floated in the centre of the room, nine tiny worlds cradled in its branches.

'It's Yggdrasil,' Lotta breathed, stepping closer. 'But really, really small.'

'Each of the Nine Worlds is unique. Following its own rules, holding its place in the world tree,' Freyja explained as a tiny volcano sent a jet of sparks into the air from Muspell.

Whetstone stared hypnotized. 'But if Loki gets his way and opens the walls . . .' The tiny tree wiggled as if in a high wind, roots and branches writhing. Worlds smashed together, seas pouring away from Midgard; dark figures slithered out of Helheim, desperately clambering from one world to another. No longer at the base of the tree, a minuscule Nidhogg the dragon beat his wings and set fire to arched temples in Vanaheim. The volcanos of Muspell crashed into the snows of Jotunheim, filling the room with ash and fog. Whetstone coughed, the air full of red sparks and smoke.

Freyja waved an arm, clearing the air and making the model of Yggdrasil vanish. 'Don't let Loki get inside your head – he's good at that. You need to stay focused.'

Lotta nodded and shuffled across the room to collect her shield from where it had been disguised as a small table. Whetstone pushed the helmet forward over his face. He hadn't forgotten about the quest; he'd just got a bit – side-tracked.

Freyja eyed his golden helmet and change of outfit sceptically. 'Simply knowing where your mother is won't make rescuing her any easier. Especially since the Giants are gathering at Utgard for one of Skrymir's feasts.'

Whetstone twitched, trying to hide his fear. Heroes weren't afraid of Giants.

'You won't find it easy getting in,' Freyja warned.

'It's getting out I'm more worried about,' Whetstone muttered, sticking his trembling fingers in his pockets. 'Any advice?'

'Yes, I'd rethink the moustache if I were you.' Freyja shook her head. 'And remember, Loki is a Fire Giant. Skrymir will help him if given the chance.'

'Frost Giants, Fire Giants – you'd think they wouldn't get on,' Whetstone mumbled, staring at his feet.

'Sometimes your differences are what make you stronger,' Freyja replied, examining her painted fingernails. 'I do not pretend to be like the other Gods, and I am more powerful because of it.'

'Dat's easy for you to say,' Lotta muttered, her voice odd.

Whetstone looked over at her and tried not to laugh. Lotta

had stuck two pieces of tissue up her nose to stop her from sneezing. Her shield blazed with colour as she pulled it on to her arm.

Freyja rolled her eyes. 'I'm trying to say, you need to be yourselves. You're stronger together than you know.'

Whetstone felt his face grow hot. Lotta looked away, tugging her sword out of a plant pot where it had been acting as a support for a large droopy flower. She tested the notched blade with her thumb. Silver droplets flowed along the blade.

'You'll just have to find it out the hard way, then.' Freyja sighed.

Lotta slipped her sword into the scabbard across her back and turned to Whetstone, the tissues wobbling. 'Right, let's get out of here.'

'One last question.' Whetstone turned back to Freyja. 'Why did you let the Valkyries smash up your hall? You could have stopped them any time you liked.'

Freyja smiled, her lips curling at the corners. 'But then I wouldn't know what they were up to. Besides, it won't take long to fix this.' Red lights filled the air; the cat hissed as all his fur stood on end. Whetstone twitched as a burst of static electricity crept over his body, making his pale skin prickle. With creaks and groans, the building began to repair itself.

A few minutes later, Lotta pushed her helmet low over her eyes and peered out of Freyja's front door. 'All clear – time to go.' Mr Tiddles wound himself around her ankles, making her twitch.

Whetstone, having changed back into his normal clothes,

nodded, and tucked his golden helmet into a cloth bag.

Freyja came forward, holding a feathery bundle. 'Just a moment. I have a couple of things which will help you.' The Goddess shook out the bundle, revealing a long cloak made of coppery feathers. Mr Tiddles swiped at it with a paw.

'Wow,' Whetstone breathed. 'Your magic cloak.'

Freyja nodded. 'With this cloak, you will be able to fly like a falcon. It will help you get to wherever you need to go.' She placed it in Whetstone's arms. The feathers tickled his skin, but the cloak itself felt like it weighed nothing.

'Thank you—'

'Don't thank me yet; you're also taking this.' From out of a pocket, the Goddess of Love and Sorcery produced –

'Ta da!' The cup jumped and spun on the palm of her hand. 'I bet you thought you would never see me again!' The cup leaped on to Lotta's shoulder.

'You need to get the cup out of Asgard.' Freyja glared at it. 'It keeps reciting the riddle, and you don't want Loki to overhear it.'

'We can take it back to Awfulrick after we've been to Jotunheim.' Lotta sniffed, her eyes still scanning the streets.

Distracted by the cloak, Whetstone ran the coppery, speckled feathers through his white fingers. 'How does it work?'

Freyja smiled. 'Put it on and you'll find out.'

Whetstone nearly dropped the cloak. 'I'm not wearing this! Lotta, you put it on!'

Lotta sighed, turning back to him. 'I don't need to; I can

already turn into a swan. It's one of the six key skills of being a Valkyrie.' Her mouth twitched into a smile. 'It's for you.'

Muttering something about misshapen ducks, Whetstone let Freyja drape the cloak around his shoulders. 'Now what?'

Freyja stepped back. 'Try to fly.'

'Just *try to fly*? No other instructions?'

Lotta looked like she was trying not to giggle. 'Think birdy thoughts.'

Whetstone turned away from the sniggering Valkyrie and giggling Goddess. Heroes would easily be able to use magic cloaks. He rolled his shoulders and stretched out his arms experimentally. With a loud *crack*, the boy vanished. In his place stood a confused-looking falcon. With another *crack*, the bird vanished, and the boy reappeared. 'What was that?!' he asked, stunned.

The cup hopped up and down on Lotta's shoulder. 'Freyja's magic cloak allows the wearer to shapeshift into a falcon, obviously,' it squeaked.

Lotta peered out into the street. 'Someone's coming. Try to fly this time.'

'What about you?' Whetstone asked, running his fingers over the cloak.

Lotta scrunched up her face and pulled her shield further up her arm. The cup jumped off her shoulder as with a *pop* and a cloud of hair, Lotta transformed into a dog. Another *pop*, and she was a girl again.

Whetstone grimaced. 'We don't have time for this!'

'Sorry. Hang on a sec.' Lotta screwed up her face again. This

67

time she turned into a bird, something between a swan and a duck. Scooping the cup up in her webbed feet, she jumped into the air. Unfortunately, before she could make it out of the room, Lotta sneezed and transformed back into a girl again. She landed with a bone-rattling thump at Whetstone's feet, the cup tumbling from her grasp. Mr Tiddles gave her a smug look. Lotta brushed cat hair off her armour and scowled.

The cup gave a jiggle and hopped over to Whetstone. 'I'm going with him.'

Lotta glared at it, retying her hair. 'Fine.'

Somewhere from outside came a shout and the sound of marching footsteps.

'Quick!' Freyja hissed. 'Get out of here!'

Whetstone nodded. He threw out his arms, knocking his helmet into his eyes. The feather cloak formed into enormous wings before shrinking down to the size of a bird. With a screech, Whetstone the Falcon jumped into the air, scrabbling for the cup as he went. He soared into the bronze sky of Asgard.

'Wait for me!' Lotta took a deep breath and crossed her arms over her chest, her shield thudding into her armour. With a flash of blue light and a flap of wings, she reappeared in mid-air as a black-and-white-speckled duck.

Whetstone swooped in front of her, a flash of copper and gold.

'Wheeee!' the cup cried, held tightly in the bird's claws.

Lotta rolled her eyes. 'Show-off.' Flapping her wings, she headed out of Freyja's Great Hall, skimming over the helmets of the approaching Valkyries before looping up and over the shining walls of Asgard. She turned into a dive, leading the way towards the snow-filled world of Jotunheim below.

A Class Three Valkyrie with one long silver plait and one silvery tuft that only reached her shoulder stepped out of formation to watch them go. Anyone looking might have noticed that her eyes weren't green and her movements not wooden like the others. She pushed her helmet back on her head and smiled. Leaving the rest of the Valkyrie platoon to face an angry Freyja and Mr Tiddles, the girl turned to jog back to Glinting-Fire at the Valkyrie Training School.

Chapter Six

Plan for Nine World Domination

The Valkyrie Training School occupied a courtyard behind Valhalla and was almost unrecognizable as the place where Lotta used to have her lessons. Grey flagstones still covered the ground, and a horse poked its head out from the line of stables, which still took up one wall. But the other walls were now decorated with blood-red flags, each embroidered with Glinting-Fire's symbol of a man held in a raven's claws.

Valkyries lined up in ranks, waiting to be given their orders. Their glittering eyes were the same colour as the magical green ice that froze their shields to a large wooden rack in the corner.

Glinting-Fire stood balanced on a stool in front of a large table that had been dragged into the centre of the space. She stabbed a finger down on to the maps of Asgard that littered its surface. 'Squadron Two, search the eastern quarter again.'

A group of Valkyries turned to jog away.

'Squadron Three, comb Idunn's orchard. They got out that way once before.'

Another group peeled away.

'They've gone,' the girl with uneven silver hair announced,

stepping into the courtyard. 'You can stop searching.'

Glinting-Fire's head shot round; tattooed lines covered her cheeks and chin. She narrowed her eyes. 'You're sure?'

Flay pulled her remaining silver plait over her shoulder and sniffed. 'I just saw them go over the wall. Lotta still can't do a swan properly; she looks more like a trampled duck.'

Glinting-Fire gave a tiny smile. 'Valkyries – stand down.'

The remaining Valkyries marched away, their green eyes flickering.

A pale girl with two long silver plaits stuck her head out from under Glinting-Fire's desk. 'It's not fair. Why does she –' the girl nodded at Flay – 'get to wander round Asgard while I have to sit here and polish everyone's shoes?'

'Because, Flee –' Flay looked down at her twin sister – 'I didn't get hit by Freyja's confusion spell and can still walk in a straight line.'

'I can walk in a straight line!' Flee put down the boot she held and crawled away from the desk. 'Watch!' She managed a couple of wobbly steps before tripping over her own feet and landing in a heap of muddy straw. A grey horse stuck his head out of the stables to snigger at her.

'Shut up,' Flay muttered to the horse as she hurried over to her sister.

Unconcerned, Flee picked straw out of her hair.

A hollow sound rang out across the courtyard. 'That's a good look for you, Flee,' said the tall, handsome man, clapping his hands. Sunbeams caught the golden threads in his tunic, making him blaze with light.

Pulling her sister out of the straw, Flay hustled her towards Loki. 'You've got magic – fix her.'

Loki paused. 'That's Freyja's magic – I can't.'

'You mean you won't,' huffed Flay, letting go of her sister's arm. 'Just like you never fixed my hair.'

'Stop talking about things you obviously do not understand,' Loki snapped. 'Different types of magic have different qualities. I cannot lift Freyja's spells, just like she cannot lift mine – otherwise she would have freed the Valkyries long ago.' He gestured to the gently glowing rack of circular shields.

Flay crossed her arms and curled her lip.

Loki glanced at Flee, who slid back under the table. 'I'm sure Freyja's spell will wear off. Eventually. You'll just have to get better at dodging.'

Glinting-Fire watched the exchange with pursed lips. 'If you two have quite finished. We've got plenty to be getting on with.' She picked up a clipboard and peered at a long list. 'We cannot afford any mistakes.'

Flay squinted, trying to read the clipboard upside down. In the Valkyrie Leader's cramped handwriting, she could just make out a title.

Glinting-Fire's Plan for Nine World Domination

The tiny Valkyrie tapped her clipboard with a pencil. 'Where were we up to?' She ran her pencil down the paper. 'Ah, *Number 27: Remove the boy and the defective Valkyrie from Freyja's protection by scaring them out of Asgard.* Check.' She ticked the paper. 'It was becoming more and more difficult to pretend that I didn't know about them,' Glinting-Fire continued with a smirk. 'If I had wanted to, my Valkyrie patrols would have dragged them back here in an instant.' Her eyes narrowed. 'Then we could have strung them up by their thumbs like the traitors they are.'

'So why didn't you?' Flee poked her silvery head out from under the desk. She gasped, her eyes wide. 'Are you scared of Freyja?'

'Impertinence!' Glinting-Fire snapped.

'We needed them to leave Asgard of their own free will,' Loki said smoothly. 'They can't take the harp string with them because of the curse, and in Jotunheim they will be friendless and alone. Freyja is too scared to go there.' Loki laid a hand on Flay's shoulder. 'She's worried the Frost Giants will try to kidnap her. Again.'

Flay shrugged the man's hand off her shoulder.

'It's all part of our strategy.' Glinting-Fire brandished her clipboard. '*Number 29: The boy and the ex-Valkyrie are captured by Skrymir and his Giants. Subsection (a): They tell us where the missing harp string is.*'

Flay's eyes followed the clipboard. 'Wait, go back a bit. How can you be sure they're going to Jotunheim? All I saw was them going over the wall.'

Flee nodded. She started counting on her fingers. 'That's right – they could be going to Alfheim or Muspell or—'

Glinting-Fire squinted at the twins. 'Do you think I've left

73

anything to chance? *Number 24: Feed Thor information about a woman who cries golden tears in Castle Utgard. Subsection (a): Ensure Thor tells everyone at Freyja's party. Subsection (b): DO NOT let Thor attempt to go and rescue the woman himself.*'

Loki's smile twisted. 'It's not easy to get things into Thor's thick skull, but once you do, they stay in there. There's no way the boy wouldn't have heard the story. Thor is about as subtle as a thrown axe.'

'Is there a bit about Odin on there?' Flay asked, craning her neck to see the clipboard. 'Isn't he in Jotunheim too?'

'Odin has been taken care of,' Loki said with a smile.

Flay narrowed her eyes. 'And Vali? How can you be sure he's on our side?'

'Vali's gone to Midgard.' Flee stuck her head out from under the desk, a black smudge across her cheek. 'I saw him on the Bifrost Bridge this morning. This jam tastes really weird,' she added, holding up a tin of boot polish. Flay snatched the tin from her sister.

Loki opened his arms wide. 'Asgard is ours.' His dark eyes gleamed. 'The trap is set, and Skrymir knows just how to treat humans who go to Castle Utgard.'

Flee nodded. 'Sausages.'

Flay tipped her head. 'So, Whetstone's mum actually *is* in Castle Utgard, and she actually *does* cry golden tears?'

Glinting-Fire sighed. '*Number 19: Acting on information received from Jotunheim, investigate presence of human woman who cries golden tears. Query: Possibly related to harp strings?* Just because we don't share all our secrets with you, Flay, doesn't mean we don't know what's going on.'

Flay scratched her nose. 'But wasn't there a whole thing about a riddle and that stupid talking cup, and—'

Loki's eyes glittered darkly. Flay gulped and stopped talking.

'Luckily it turned out that Skrymir was indeed holding the woman and the harp string prisoner.' Glinting-Fire turned over a page on her clipboard. 'He agreed to swap his prize for the opportunity to free the Frost Giants from Jotunheim.'

Flee sniffed. 'I don't blame him – I wouldn't want to stay in Jotunheim either. It's a dump.' Flay gave her a kick under the table.

Glinting-Fire licked her pencil. She glanced at Loki. 'You have moved the woman?'

'Yes, yes.' Loki examined his fingernails. 'She was only too happy to make a deal too: the harp string in exchange for her return to Midgard.' The corners of his lips turned up. 'Such a shame she didn't think to specify exactly *where* in Midgard.'

Flee picked polish out from under her fingernails. 'Why? Where did you take her?'

Loki just grinned.

'So, what next?' Flay put her hands on her hips. 'Whetstone and Lotta are in Jotunheim, but they know you won't be far behind.' She nodded at Loki. 'They'll be expecting a trick. They have met you, you know.'

'It's a trick, it's a trick. It's a trickity-trick-trick,' said a voice from under the table. 'Whetstone goes to Jotunheim to find his mum and her harp string.' Flee's head popped out;

75

she flapped her arms like wings. 'But oh no! –' her fingers splayed across her cheeks – 'Loki's got there first and moved her to Midgard. Now they're going to be eaten by Giants!' She mimed cooking sausages on a frying pan. '*Please don't eat us – we'll tell you everything you want to know! Too late – it's sausage time!*'

Flay's nose wrinkled as Flee voiced both the Giants and a tiny Whetstone and Lotta. 'Wow, that spell has really messed you up.'

Flee started to giggle.

Loki looked down his nose at the girl pretending to eat talking sausages. 'The boy has a way of wiggling out of things. He wouldn't willingly tell the Giants where the last harp string is, but he might tell someone he trusts.'

Flay stuck out her lip in thought. She pulled her plait over her shoulder. 'Oh! Is it *Number 30: Loki to shapeshift into Whetstone's mum and get the information out of him that way?*'

Loki smiled. 'I have a more *interesting* idea.' He looked at the girl appraisingly.

Flay looked from Loki to Glinting-Fire and back again. 'What? *What!*'

Chapter Seven

Heroes Don't Play Tea Parties

Lotta the Duck stretched out her webbed feet, landing with a long skid on a frozen lake. Behind her, Whetstone the Falcon crash-landed in a snowdrift. The cup hopped out and shook snowflakes away from its jewels.

Back in his human form, Whetstone's scruffy head poked out of the snow. 'Brrrr! It's freezing!'

With a flash of blue light, Lotta transformed back into a Valkyrie. 'Landing is always the worst part. You have to sort of go up and down at the same time.'

Whetstone pulled himself out of the snow. He wrapped the feathery cloak around his shoulders and shivered. 'Why can't we ever go anywhere warm?'

Lotta straightened her hairy socks, her skin a warm copper against the white snow. 'Don't blame me. Next time your family gets cursed, let's hope

one of them ends up in Muspell.' Gazing into the sky, she added, 'I don't think we were followed, but we should probably move.' She looked around at the snow-filled landscape. 'Where in Jotunheim do we have to go?'

Whetstone checked he still had the bag with his helmet. 'Erm, Castle Utgard.'

'Castle Utgard? The main settlement of the Giants?' Lotta spluttered. 'A terrifying fortress of ice and stone ruled by the Frost Giant Skrymir, where no Gods, Valkyries or humans dare to tread?'

'I suppose I should also tell you that Freyja said Skrymir is having some sort of feast, so there will be more Giants than ever.' Whetstone bared his teeth in a forced smile.

Lotta threw up her hands. 'Fine, fine. That's perfect.' She put her hands on her hips. 'And what is your plan for when we get there? Walk in and ask if they've got a woman who cries golden tears hanging around?'

Whetstone pulled the bag over his shoulder. 'That's what a real Hero would do.'

'Right, yes. Excellent. You do realize that all these "real Heroes" you've been copying are dead, don't you?'

Whetstone squinted against the light bouncing off the snow. 'Look, there's something over there.' He pointed at a dark shape. 'I'm going to see what it is.' He trudged off.

Lotta plucked the golden cup out of the snow. 'I don't suppose you've got any ideas?'

The cup gazed up at her with ruby eyes. 'Don't ask me – you picked him up. You could've chosen a proper Hero and not had any of these problems.'

Lotta caught up with Whetstone as he came to a halt in front of a curved dark object as high as his shoulder. 'What is that?'

'I think – it's a bucket.'

The wooden bucket was lying on its side, half buried in snow. Whetstone reached out to touch the dark wood. 'I know this is the Land of the Giants, I just didn't expect things to be so—'

'Giant?' A loud crunching came from behind them. 'Quick!' Lotta hissed. 'Get inside before we get stepped on!'

Together they crouched awkwardly inside the bucket as the footsteps got closer. A shadow passed over them.

Suddenly the bucket was tipped upright, throwing Whetstone and Lotta backwards into its snowy depths. Whetstone spluttered his way to the surface, still wrapped in the feathered cloak. Lotta's feet stuck

out of the snow next to him. Whetstone plunged his hand down, hoping to help pull her out. Lotta emerged, coughing, the cup still clutched in her hand. 'What's happening?' it whined.

Whetstone's stomach rolled as the bucket was lifted into the air. Above them and holding the bucket's handle was an enormous blue-skinned hand. The hand extended into an arm, which vanished into a shadowy figure. 'Giant!' Whetstone squeaked.

The Frost Giant paused, then, peering down, shrieked, 'MOUSE!'

The bucket flew through the air, Lotta and Whetstone tumbling out to land face first in the snow. Whetstone rolled out of the way as the bucket crashed down beside them. The Giant hopped about, shrieking.

Lotta sat up, shaking snow out of her face. 'OI!' she bellowed. 'STOP THAT! YOU'LL CRUSH US!'

The Giant paused, looking around. 'Mousey? Can you talk?'

'WE'RE NOT MICE!' Lotta bellowed again, climbing out of the snow. Standing, she was only slightly taller than the Giant's ankle. 'STOP CHUCKING US ABOUT!' Whetstone put his hands over his ears before he was deafened.

An enormous face loomed over them. Pale blue fingers brushed a white fringe out of the eyes of a young girl in an embroidered apron. She peered at them curiously. 'Are you dollies?' A huge finger poked Whetstone in the chest, knocking him over.

'Get off,' he spluttered. 'We're not toys.'

A massive hand reached down and grabbed Lotta round the middle; a second hand picked up Whetstone. The boy struggled in her grasp, trying to free himself but not wanting to fall at the same time. The Giant lifted them up to eye height. Frost sparkled in her eyelashes; freckles the colour of pebbles covered her blue cheeks. 'You're so cute!' she squealed. Whetstone gasped as all the air was squeezed out of him.

Held tight in the Giant's hand, Lotta struggled to free her arms. 'Listen, little girl. Have you ever seen anyone our size before?'

The girl Giant nodded. She turned to point at the horizon. Whetstone felt his stomach whoosh as he was waved through the air. 'Grandpa's got one in a cage. He lets me play tea parties with her sometimes.'

Whetstone's insides did more somersaults, and not

82

through queasiness this time. She must be talking about his mum.

Lotta nodded. 'Good. What's your grandpa's name?'

The girl shrugged. 'Grandpa?'

'Never mind. Do you know where we are?'

The Frost Giant straightened up proudly. 'This is Utgard.'

Lotta grimaced. 'Of course. We would really like to visit the woman in the cage. Do you think you could take us to see her – without any of the other Giants seeing us?'

The girl tipped her head, her blue nose scrunched up in thought. 'I'm not supposed keep secrets.'

'But,' Lotta invented, 'if anyone sees us, they might lock us up in a cage too, and then we wouldn't be able to play with you.'

The girl stuck out her lip.

'Gert? What are you doing out there?' shouted a loud voice.

Gert thrust her hands behind her back; Whetstone and Lotta narrowly avoided being smashed together.

'It's nearly time for the feast.'

'Coming!' Gert yelled. Turning away, she shoved Whetstone and Lotta into her apron pocket. 'Stay there,' she whispered, patting the pocket and nearly flattening Lotta. 'We can play tea parties in my bedroom later.'

'Heroes don't play tea parties,' Whetstone huffed.

'This is not what I imagined doing when I said I was going to be a proper Hero.' Whetstone pouted. He looked down at the doll-sized cups and saucers in front of him. He was sat on a pile of books in between a pink teddy bear and a naked rag doll. Lotta sat opposite him, the rag doll's dress forced on over her armour.

The golden cup twirled on the table in front of them. 'I think it's sweet. She just wants to play.'

Across the room, Gert hummed as she laid out imaginary cakes and sandwiches on a plate.

'Stop complaining. We're in the castle, aren't we?' Lotta pulled at the dress; the ruffles and bows at odds with her armour.

Gert placed a tray down on the table in front of them. She picked up a teapot. 'Tea, Mrs Magnuson?'

Lotta gave her a big grin.

'Gert, who are you talking to?' asked a boy's voice. The bedroom door creaked open.

'No one!' Gert squealed, leaping forward. 'It's a secret – get out!'

Lotta caught Whetstone's eye. 'Just stay still,' she hissed, freezing in position. 'I have a plan.'

A larger boy Giant pushed his way in and scanned the room.

'Get out, Thom! You're not allowed in my room! Mum! *Mum!*'

'Stupid tea parties,' the boy muttered, flicking the table over with his toe. Lotta's face froze as an enormous hand reached down towards her. 'This one is new.'

Whetstone swung the bag containing his helmet into the boy's ankle. 'Hop it, Giant!' It connected with a crunching sound.

'Argh!'

Lotta snatched up the magic cup as the Giant boy jumped around, clutching his leg.

'They're real! I'm telling Mum – you're not allowed—'

'You couldn't just do what I said, could you?' Lotta stuffed the cup into Whetstone's bag and started dragging him towards the door. 'Now everyone is going to know we're here, genius!'

In the corridor a huge woman shrieked at the sight of them, tossing the tray she carried into the air. Enormous lumps of mashed turnip rained down. Whetstone jumped over the woman's foot and together he and Lotta sped towards the far end of the corridor. It hadn't seemed that far carried in Gert's pocket, but now it went on endlessly. Finally they skidded through an open doorway and found themselves in a steamy kitchen.

'I bet you're missing the tea party now!' Lotta panted as she drew her sword. Silver drops ran up and down the blade.

Frost Giants turned to stare at the commotion. Blue skin, purple or white hair, and heavy boots. Someone aimed a kick at Whetstone. 'Get them!' shouted someone else.

Lotta lifted her shield, but before she could do anything,

the world around Whetstone went dark. A large saucepan slammed over him, knocking him sideways.

'Got you!'

Whetstone's ears rung from the impact. He climbed to his knees, fingers feeling for the base of the pan.

Lotta hammered on the side of the saucepan. 'Let him out!' A screech followed as someone grabbed her. Whetstone's chest felt tight. He tried not to panic.

With a scraping noise, the pan lifted slightly and something poked underneath. A piece of paper nudged up against Whetstone's knees. The boy had to shuffle on top of it so it didn't knock him over.

'Careful, don't let it escape,' said a gruff voice.

Whetstone gasped as the saucepan was flipped over, the paper now a lid rather than a floor. The cup grunted as Whetstone landed on it. Whetstone's stomach dropped as the pan swooped through the air before being placed gently on a flat surface.

'Are you ready?' asked a muffled voice. Someone murmured in response.

Whetstone sat up as the paper was lifted away. Four blue-skinned faces peered down at him. Each face was longer than he was tall. Dark blue eyes framed by white lashes, noses the size of his leg. Whetstone tried to grin; it felt like a rictus on his face. 'So, I suppose you're wondering what I'm doing here?'

Lotta's brown face appeared over the edge of the saucepan. She wrinkled her nose.

'What do we do?' Whetstone hissed, still staring up at the Frost Giants. His skin clammy with fear and nausea.

'You should probably start by getting out of the saucepan. Haven't you heard what Giants do to humans?' Lotta rolled her eyes.

Whetstone snatched up his bag and scrambled out to stand next to the girl, who shifted away slightly. If he didn't want to end up as breakfast, he had to convince the Giants he was a Hero. Whetstone tried to stand up straight and push his chest out.

The cup peeked out. 'They're going to eat us!'

Whetstone rammed it back into the bag, pulling out the helmet instead.

'I am Rhett the Bone-Breaker,' the boy announced, trying to keep the tremor out of his voice. He shoved the helmet on his head, the wonky eyeholes making it difficult to see. 'Single Combat Champion of Valhalla! I perform mighty quests, save the innocent, defeat monsters . . . that sort of thing.'

'You what?' Lotta muttered, tossing her curls. 'Shut up.'

'What's the matter?' Whetstone hissed, pushing the helmet into place. 'Are things not going to *plan*? You're supposed to be helping me.'

After a moment, Lotta plastered a wide grin on her face. She stepped away and opened her arms. 'Ladies and Gentle Giants,' she began with a flourish. 'I, Lotta the disgraced trainee Valkyrie, on the run from Asgard, and therefore *totally* trustworthy, would like to introduce the mighty Hero – *What was your name again?*' she added in a loud whisper.

'Rhett the Bone-Breaker,' Whetstone replied, stunned.

'Wow. Are you sure?' Lotta gave him a disbelieving look. 'Cos you look like the only bones you could break are your own.'

As Whetstone spluttered, an elderly Giant woman elbowed her way forward, wispy white hair escaping from under a headscarf. 'If that one *is* a Hero –' she pointed a shaky finger at Whetstone – 'we should tell Lord Skrymir. He knows how to deal with Heroes.' Whetstone stared hypnotized at a large wart which wobbled on her chin.

Lotta crossed her arms. 'Yeah, do that. But warn him that

Heroes aren't as impressive as they used to be.'

'Lotta, what is wrong with you?' Whetstone hissed.

'No one is going to believe you're a real Hero.' Lotta poked the helmet, making it slip sideways. 'Cop on to yourself.'

'I am a real Hero.' Whetstone pushed the helmet out of his eyes. 'You saw me in Valhalla.'

'Fine.' Lotta huffed. 'Just don't blame me when this all goes wrong.'

'A *real Hero* in Jotunheim,' interjected a Giant, rubbing his bushy beard. 'I can't remember when that last happened.'

A purple-haired woman nodded. 'And just in time for the feast.'

Gert wiggled her way to the front. She pulled her thumb out of her mouth with a *pop*. 'Can I keep them as pets? Pleeeease! I promise I'll look after them.' The purple-haired woman shushed her.

'I'm sure Lord Skrymir would invite such a mighty Hero to the feast as his *special guest*,' the bearded Giant said with a slow smile.

'Special ingredient, more like,' Lotta muttered.

Whetstone grinned up at the blue faces watching him. 'Excuse us just a moment.' He dragged Lotta across the table and behind a stack of plates. 'Look, I know you never believed I could really be a Hero, but we need them –' he gestured at the Giants – 'to believe in me, otherwise they might eat us. And you –' Lotta wrenched her arm out of his grasp – 'are messing everything up.'

Lotta tossed her head but said nothing.

'We have to find my mum and get the harp string, and if we play nice with the Giants, maybe they'll, I dunno, give us a clue or some information or something.'

Lotta pulled at her black curls, trying to stretch them over her shoulder, but realized they were too short. She fluffed her bunches instead. 'Oh yeah, the precious harp strings. How could I forget.'

'Is there a problem?' asked the bearded Giant, lifting the plates out of the way.

Whetstone narrowed his eyes at Lotta. 'No.'

'Excellent –' the Giant lowered a pale blue hand to the table for Whetstone to step on to – 'I'll bring you to Lord Skrymir.'

The boy gulped, gazing up at the huge blue faces surrounding him. Suddenly all he could focus on was their massive teeth. Fear churned in his stomach. Freyja's words came back to him: if the Frost Giants found out who he really was, they would tell Loki, and Loki would get the harp string first.

With a sigh, Lotta brushed past him and on to the Giant's hand. 'Too late for second thoughts. Let's get on with it.' She sat down and crossed her arms.

Whetstone took a deep breath. The Giants thought he was a Hero, so he'd better give them a Hero.

Chapter Eight

A Feast at Castle Utgard

There once was a Hero named Rhett,
Who was the best you ever can get –

The cup's voice cut through the sounds of Giants chewing, arguing and feasting. Bowls and platters of food covered every table. Meat, vegetables, stews, even a big wobbly jelly.

He's the greatest by far,
Such a superstar.
Now you've met him, you'll never forget!

The cup wasn't having any problems making up poems about Rhett the Bone-Breaker, despite the fact that he had only been invented that afternoon and had been on no amazing adventures and hadn't performed any Heroic acts.

Up on the top table, Whetstone sat in place of honour next to Skrymir. The Frost Giant sat on a sturdy chair, but being so small, Whetstone sat on the table itself beside the enormous wooden plates. He had always wanted to be invited to dine at the top table – that was where the most important people sat. But having grown up in a home for orphaned wolf cubs run by his foster mother, Angrboda, it had never happened. Most people just wanted to avoid his fleas.

'A toast to our guest,' Skrymir bellowed, making Whetstone nearly fall into a bowl of pickled onions. 'Rhett the Bone-Breaker!'

Whetstone pushed his helmet out of his eyes and picked up the thimble he had been using as a cup; it was good being a proper Hero like Rhett. This was why things had gone wrong in Helheim and he had been forced to leave his father there. *Whetstone* had tried to rescue him. If it had been *Rhett*, everything would have gone smoothly.

'Rhett the Bone-Breaker,' the Giants chorused.

Whetstone stood up and shouted over the noise. 'Thank you. It's a great feast.'

Skrymir nodded. He was a powerfully built man, with a broad chest and long white hair, which fell around his shoulders. His pale blue skin twinkled against the deep purple tunic he wore.

Lotta sat scowling on the table beside Whetstone. Whetstone ignored her; she had been in a foul mood since the feast started, when he'd caught her staring at her reflection in a bowl of soup. He knew she wasn't the greatest fan of Rhett the Bone-Breaker, but she didn't normally mope. Maybe she'd hurt herself when the Giants caught them?

Lotta poked him with a piece of broken carrot stick. 'Figured out where your mum is yet?'

Whetstone took another drink. 'I can't decide how to ask without them getting suspicious.'

'Ha.'

'Besides, it's rude to sneak out in the middle of a feast.' Whetstone didn't want to admit it, and especially not to Lotta in the mood she was in, but he was quite enjoying being Rhett and was in no rush to leave.

Lotta tipped her head. 'But seriously, aren't you even a bit worried that Thor will tell Loki where your mum is before you find her?' Her eyes were fixed on his face.

Whetstone looked away, uncomfortable. 'Loki doesn't know about the riddle, so he won't know it's my mum.'

'No, but maybe he'll figure it out another way.' Lotta sat back. 'After what happened in Helheim, I thought you'd be desperate to get there first.'

Whetstone shrugged, not answering.

'It must feel weird not wearing your dad's harp string any more.' The girl eyed the collar of his shirt, before flicking her eyes back to his face. 'Are you sure it's safe – up in –' Lotta's eyes narrowed – 'Asgard?'

Accompanied by the cup, a table of Giants started to chant a song Whetstone had once heard the Vikings sing on Midgard.

> *Asgard! Asgard!*
> *Your time will soon be done!*
> *No more Asgard!*
> *When the Frost Giants come!*

Whetstone wasn't sure what the Gods would think of this new version.

Lotta's brown eyes bored into his face. 'If *I* was you, I would want to find my mum and get back to – Freyja's – as soon as possible. That way I would have two harp strings.'

Freyja's the most beautiful of all,

warbled the Giants.

And one day she will be ours!
We'll steal her out of Asgard,
Cos all the Gods are cowards!

'Don't you think Skrymir will notice if we suddenly vanish?' Whetstone muttered, looking away from Lotta's intense gaze. 'He'll wonder where we're going.'

A smirk crossed Lotta's face. 'I wouldn't worry about that.'

Asgard! Asgard!
Your time will soon be done!

the Giants crooned.

No more Asgard!
When the Frost Giants come!

'Honestly, I don't see what all the fuss is about the Frost Giants,' Whetstone muttered, pulling his helmet back down over his face. 'They've been really nice so far.'

Lotta rolled her eyes. 'Yeah, so nice. Whetstone, your *literal* mum is in a *literal* cage. Or something.' She tried to stretch her hair over her shoulder again. 'Rescuing her is *literally* what we are here for,' she added, combing her fingers through her black curls instead. 'Besides, the sooner we find your mum, the sooner I can get out of here.'

Whetstone wrinkled his brow. 'You mean *we* can get out of here?'

Lotta gave him a blank stare. 'That's what I said. Plus, Loki is looking for you, or have you forgotten that?'

Loki's the one they call Trickster;

One Giant had climbed on to the bench, waving his tankard to conduct the singing.

He's a Fire Giant – he's one of us!
He'll help us win at Ragnarok,
When we'll grind all the Gods into dust!

Whetstone gave a shudder. 'Loki is still in Asgard. Freyja said she would let us know if he left.' He peered at Lotta carefully. 'Or have *you* forgotten *that*?'

Lotta snorted. 'Freyja thinks she's so great, but what can she do really? Her magic is rubbish – it can't even free the Valkyries from Loki's spell.'

'I wondered about that.' Whetstone had to almost shout over the singing Giants. 'So, her magic can't affect Loki's?'

Lotta tossed her head. 'Only a Giant can break another Giant's magic, dummy. Freyja is a Goddess – she can only lift spells cast by another God or Goddess.'

'Right. So, you need to get another Giant to help you free the Valkyries. Any ideas who?'

Lotta sniffed. 'The Valkyries are fine as they are.' She saw his look and added, 'For the time being. Until I figure everything out. Which I'm working on. Right now.'

'OK,' Whetstone said slowly.

Asgard! Asgard!
Your time will soon be done!

The Giants stamped their feet in a crescendo.

No more Asgard!
When the Frost Giants come!

Around them, the Giants erupted into cheers as their song ended. Lotta hesitated, then whacked Whetstone on the arm, a sour look flashed across her face. 'Come on.' Shaking her head and muttering, Lotta clambered down from the table.

'Where are you going?' Whetstone asked, confused.

'I can't sit around here all day,' she called back. 'Someone has got to do the job you're supposed to be doing!'

Whetstone slumped. Something was very wrong with Lotta, but – she was right. Sitting around feasting with Giants wasn't getting them any closer to the harp string. He pulled the helmet off his head and turned it over in his hands. He needed to find his mum before Loki turned up – unless . . . he was here already? Whetstone watched the trainee Valkyrie pick her way through the forest of Giant feet and legs. His eyes narrowed as she did that funny movement again where she tried to stretch her hair over her shoulder.

He shook the thought out of his head. Castle Utgard must be making her twitchy; it probably reminded her too much of Helheim as they were both cold and snowy.

He shoved the helmet back into the bag and grabbed the cup as it bopped past.

'Are we off? I was enjoying myself,' the cup complained.

'We've got stuff to do.' Whetstone shuffled to the edge of the table.

'Hero stuff?'

'Something like that.'

Skrymir tapped his fingers thoughtfully on his goblet as he watched Whetstone follow the trainee Valkyrie towards the door and out into the corridor beyond.

Whetstone trotted after Lotta along the gloomy corridor. She strode quickly, her boots landing lightly on the enormous flagstones. 'Are you all right? No offence, Lotta, but you're acting kind of strange.'

Lotta sniffed. 'I don't know what you're taking about.' Her walk changed, her feet now thumping down in a sort of march.

The cup wobbled on Whetstone's shoulder. 'Where are we going?' it asked.

'Be quiet,' Lotta hissed. 'No one is talking to you!'

'Well, excuse me,' the cup whined, its voice bouncing off the stone walls. 'I was only asking a question. Surely I'm allowed to ask questions.'

'This way.' Holding her glowing shield like a torch, Lotta led them around a corner and along another equally gloomy corridor. A lantern flickered against the stone wall. Its light didn't reach all the way to the floor, but it was a point of brightness in the shadows.

Whetstone scuttled behind Lotta. 'How do you know where to go?'

'I don't.' Lotta slowed down, her dark skin gleaming with

the shield's colours. 'But if your mum cries golden tears, the Giants are bound to have her somewhere secure, probably in the centre of the castle.' She made a show of looking around. 'Hmmmm. This way.' She marched off stiffly.

'Did Lotta get a personality transplant while I wasn't looking?' the cup asked. 'Because this is not the grumpy trainee Valkyrie we've come to know.'

'I'm sure she's fine,' Whetstone said slowly. 'She's probably just in a mood because we aren't following a plan.'

Lotta paused, waiting for them to catch up. 'So, remind me,' she said, her eyes scanning the corridor. 'The three harp strings. You found the one your dad was holding when the curse struck.' Whetstone nodded slowly. 'Your mum, who is somewhere in this castle, has a second one. And the third one . . .'

'Loki knows where it is,' Whetstone said flatly.

'And your dad's one is still up in Asgard?' Lotta continued.

'Why do you keep asking me that? You know where it is.'

Lotta sniffed. 'Of course I do. I was just making conversation.' She lifted the shield, its lights reflecting off the stone walls. 'Hypothetically, if you were going to hide something in Asgard, where would you put it?'

Whetstone stopped to stare at her. 'You tell me.'

Lotta paused at the end of the corridor. She turned back to Whetstone with a smile plastered on her face. 'Which way do you think we should go?'

Whetstone sidled closer. 'I dunno.' He peered both ways along the corridor: the walls were lined with doors. Whetstone's heart sank. 'This is going to take forever. I told you we should have stayed at the feast – Skrymir might have said something. Or maybe we should have asked Gert for directions.'

'Who's Gert?'

Whetstone goggled at her. 'Seriously? The tea party, the bucket, she made you wear that dress?'

'Oh yeah. Gert.' Lotta tossed her head.

'I've got an idea,' said the cup from where it sat on Whetstone's shoulder. Before anyone could reply, it yelled at the top of its metallic voice, 'Cooee! Anyone human in here?' From the feast came the sound of a plate clattering to the floor and startled voices.

Whetstone grabbed hold of the cup, wrapping his hands around its mouth. 'What are you doing? They're going to notice we've gone!'

Lotta reached for her sword, but then spun around as a soft voice called out, 'Hello?'

The cup slipped from Whetstone's stunned fingers. He twisted around on the spot, trying to figure out which door the voice had come from. The cup landed on the flagstones with a clang.

'Is someone there?' the soft voice continued, hesitantly. 'I'm a human.'

'This way!' squeaked the cup. It bounced towards a huge, heavily barred door. 'I told you my ideas were always brilliant. I don't know how you manage without me.'

Whetstone placed a hand on the painted wood of the enormous door, his heart thumping in his chest, his worries about Lotta's odd behaviour swept away by a tide of excitement and nervousness. That had to be his mum; she was just behind this door. 'How do we get in?' He gazed up at the keyhole high above them. 'Are you any good at picking locks?'

Lotta waggled her shield. 'I'm a Valkyrie, not a criminal.'

Whetstone ran his hands over the thick wood. 'Why don't you use your sword to cut a hole in the door?'

Lotta's expression froze for a second, then she smiled her odd smile again. 'Ye-es, I can do that because I have magic powers and a magic sword.' Holding the shield in one hand, slowly she pulled the long sword out of its scabbard and over her shoulder.

Whetstone watched the blade, waiting for the silver droplets to appear like always. Lotta swung the sword out in front of her, her jaw clenched as if she was worried it would explode.

Whetstone's eyes flicked to Lotta's grim face. 'What are you waiting for? My mum is inside!'

'Erm –' Lotta lowered the blade, her eyes darting around – 'I don't think we should use the sword, because –' her eyes fixed on something in the shadows – 'we can use that mousehole instead.'

'Ooh, good one.' The cup hopped towards a crack in the wall.

Lotta sheathed the blade. 'After you. *Hero*.'

Whetstone hesitated.

'Please help me,' called the voice again. It was definitely coming from inside the room.

'Go on,' Lotta hissed, her expression strange in the light

from the shield. 'Aren't Heroes supposed to save damsels in distress?'

Whetstone nodded and shoved the helmet back on to his head. Taking a deep breath, he wiggled through the narrow gap following the cup.

❦

Inside, the room was dark. A single candle sat on top of a tall table. Something glittered beside it.

The words of the riddle ran through Whetstone's head:

> *The other you will find, bound by a glittering chain.*
> *She is kept for her tears, they fall as golden rain.*

'Hello?' Lotta called into the gloom. 'Anyone there?'

'Yes, me!' replied the voice. A gentle clinking followed, and a hand, pale against the darkness, waved from the top of the table. 'I've been here so long – let me out. Please!'

Whetstone's heart thumped heavily in his chest. He could be about to see his mother for the first time in twelve years. Butterflies fluttered in his stomach. He swallowed back his nerves, telling himself his mum was bound to be impressed by Rhett the Bone-Breaker. Fumbling for the edges of the falcon cloak, he sucked in a breath, feeling the cool air fill up his lungs, his eyes fixed on the glittering lights.

Lotta put her hand on his arm. 'Wait, the harp string, up in Asgard – remind me where it is again?'

Whetstone felt his butterflies turn to ice cubes. He couldn't ignore her odd behaviour or pretend it was just nerves any longer. Lotta would never ask so many questions about the harp string. She was the one who hid it; she's the only one who knew where it was. Whetstone turned to face the girl next to him, his fingers clenching on the feathers of his cloak. Lotta wouldn't have forgotten about Gert. Lotta wouldn't have insulted Freyja or been unable to use her magic sword. There was only one explanation: this girl wasn't Lotta.

'It's with Freyja, isn't it? She's looking after it for you,' the girl asked, opening her brown eyes wide.

Whetstone's palms started to sweat. He let go of the cloak and wiped his hands on his trousers.

The girl moved towards him. 'Why won't you tell me?' She fluttered her thick eyelashes. 'We're friends, aren't we? Don't you trust me?'

Whetstone paused, the temptation to tell this girl that the harp string was in Mr Tiddles' cat basket or Thor's underwear drawer almost overwhelming. That would give him a chance to find his mum and the real Lotta while they were searching in the wrong places. But lying wasn't very Heroic . . .

A muffled clinking came from above them. 'Hello! Anyone down there?' called the voice. 'I want to get out now.'

Whetstone took a step back, his chin raised. 'I trust Lotta. But you're not Lotta, are you – *Loki*?'

The girl's brown face scrunched up like she had just bitten into a lemon. 'What?! I am *not* Loki!'

Whetstone blinked in surprise. Loki was a shapeshifter;

he would be able to disguise himself as Lotta easily, but her reaction seemed a bit too genuine. 'Huh?'

The girl stamped her foot. 'I cannot *believe* you would think I was that slimy Trickster.' From above them came the sound of someone giggling. 'I have never been so insulted,' Lotta continued.

'I'm sorry – I . . .' Whetstone's mouth opened and closed as he sought to find the right words. He had been so sure that this wasn't really Lotta. 'But why were you acting so strange? And what was with all those questions about the harp string? You hid it – I don't even know where it is!'

'WHAT! You don't *know* where it is!' The girl let out a growl of frustration, her fingers twisting into claws. 'I have had enough of this.' She ground her teeth. With a loud *crack* and a flash of light, the Valkyrie transformed into a sleek-looking swan. Angrily flapping her wings, she took off, heading for the tabletop.

'Wait, Lotta! Stop!'

The cup bopped past. 'Wow, that didn't go so well.'

Whetstone snatched it up. 'But even you said she wasn't acting right!' he said, giving it a little shake.

'What do I know? I'm a cup.'

Thoroughly confused, Whetstone shoved the golden cup and his helmet back into his bag before transforming into a falcon and flying up to join the girl on the table.

Chapter Nine

Double Trouble

With a wobble, Whetstone landed on the table behind Lotta and transformed back into a boy. 'I'm sorry –' he puffed. 'When did you get the hang . . . of . . . swans?' His voice faltered as he took in the sparkling object on the table.

A metal bird cage as big as a house towered over them. Candlelight glinted off golden bars as thick as Whetstone's arm.

'*She is kept for her tears, they fall as golden rain,*' Whetstone murmured to himself, placing the bag on the floor.

The cup popped out. '*Why are you talking like that? Are you feeling the strain?*'

Whetstone ignored it, he inched closer. A glittering chain with a heavy padlock looped around the cage, keeping the door securely closed. His mouth went dry. After twelve years of being kept apart by a curse, he was about to see his mum. Whetstone wrapped his hands around two of the bars, his heart thumping.

Before Whetstone could react, the cup jumped through the bars. 'Is this a house or a birdcage?' it asked, clattering against the metal floor. 'Look, there's a swing, a perch and even a mirror.'

'Get back here,' Whetstone hissed.

The cup bobbed about admiring its reflection. Long cracks criss-crossed the glass and one pointy shard was missing. 'Who's a pretty cup then?' A dark shape moved inside the mirror. 'Wait, that's not me.'

'It's a mirror-door,' Lotta explained, stepping behind Whetstone. He could feel her hot breath on his cheek. 'Or it was, before it got smashed. Made with Giant magic.'

'Ooh, they're rare,' the cup squealed.

'So, my mum's not here?' Whetstone swallowed, forcing down the crushing disappointment. 'She went out through

107

this mirror?' He scrunched up his forehead. 'But then, whose voice did we hear?'

A shadow separated itself from behind the birdcage, candlelight picking out the gold in his hair and tunic.

'Loki.' Whetstone's fingers tightened around the bars of the cage, his knees wobbling.

Loki sauntered forward. 'Your mother is safe, Whetstone. She's gone to stay with a friend of mine.'

'Bring her back.' Heat prickled across Whetstone's skin. Anger surged through him. He had been so close, just for Loki to mess everything up again.

Loki trailed his fingers across the golden bars. 'I can't. Your mother broke the mirror after we passed through. I think she wanted to ensure no one could put her in the cage again.'

Whetstone clenched his jaw so tightly he thought his teeth might crack.

'Your mother was *so* pleased that *someone* had come to rescue her,' Loki added. 'I don't think she would appreciate her *son* bringing her back here.'

Blood pounded in Whetstone's head.

'She was so grateful,' Loki continued as he moved around the cage, stripes of light blazing off his hair and fine clothes, 'that she was happy to give me this in exchange for taking her back to Midgard.' Whetstone felt the sting of bile in his throat as he watched Loki curl the harp string around his fingers. His own fingers flew to his neck where his father's harp string used to be.

'What a curious power. The first harp string warns of danger – I can see that might be useful.' Loki continued twisting the glowing string around his fingers. 'The second can change someone's appearance. But golden tears?'

'Wait, you said the second string can change appearances.' Whetstone stepped away from the cage, his hands clenching into fists. 'That one was mine?'

Loki laughed. 'Oh yes, the harp string left behind with you on Midgard. Angrboda's been looking after it for me.'

'The Angry Bogey,' Whetstone repeated under his breath, his fingernails leaving grooves in his palms. 'Let me guess, that's the *friend* you took my mum to?'

Loki tucked the glowing string deep into a pocket. 'I have this harp string, and Angrboda will give me the second.' He fixed his dark eyes on Whetstone. 'Tell me where the last harp string is, and I'll bring you to your mother.'

'Don't waste your time.' Lotta stomped up to the bars and gave one a kick, making the cage vibrate unpleasantly; the cup fell over with a jingle. 'This whole thing has been pointless. He doesn't know where the harp string is.'

Loki's eyes narrowed.

Lotta rounded the cage and marched towards Loki. 'He can't tell us anything – *he* didn't hide his dad's harp string.' She turned to point through the bars. '*She* did.'

A giggle came from the back of the cage. 'Can we come out now?' sang a girl's voice. 'I'm bored of hiding.'

A chill swept up Whetstone's spine. He dragged his eyes away from Loki's face, straining to see who else lurked in the darkness. Lotta wouldn't have told anyone else where the harp string was, would she?

The cup righted itself. 'Is that your mum? She sounds younger than I expected.'

Whetstone backed away as a girl with pale skin and long silver plaits appeared in the candlelight. 'What's going on? You didn't hide the harp string, Frieda, Felicity, er . . .'

'Flee.' The girl grinned.

A cold lump formed in Whetstone's chest.

'Not me – I'm a "danger to myself",' explained the girl, waggling her fingers. 'And need "keeping an eye on". That's why they left me in here.' She pulled a blanket off a lumpy shape huddled next to her. 'You're talking about *her*.'

Whetstone gasped as from under the blanket a familiar face appeared, a gag tied around her mouth and heavy ropes pinning her arms to her sides. 'Lotta?' Whetstone's eyes flicked from the Lotta outside the birdcage to the one inside it.

Inside the cage, Flee giggled, pointing at the Lottas. 'Uh-oh, double trouble!'

Whetstone reeled backwards, his thoughts spinning. 'I knew there was something wrong with you!' He pointed at the girl beside Loki. 'You kept doing that thing with your hair.'

The girl sniffed. 'Pathetic.' She kicked the bars again. 'Loki, turn me back.'

With a wave of Loki's hand, a ripple of light travelled up the girl next to him. As the light passed over her, she changed. Pale skin, silver hair and a sneering expression.

Flee clapped her hands. 'Flay, yay! Hey, that rhymes.'

Inside the cage, the real Lotta fixed her eyes on Whetstone. 'I cannot believe you thought she was me, even for a second!' she hissed, managing to free herself from the gag.

Whetstone scraped his white hand through his hair. 'You were identical!'

'She looked nothing like me!'

Flay faced Whetstone, her arms crossed. 'And I can't believe you thought *I* was Loki. Moron.'

'But – but –' Whetstone stammered.

'The harp string is somewhere in Asgard,' Flay continued, turning back to Loki. 'That's as much as he knows.' She dumped Lotta's glowing shield on the floor. Using the tips of her fingers, she pulled the notched sword out of her scabbard. 'Yeuch, get this thing away from me.' She dropped it to the tabletop with a clang. Inside the cage, Lotta eyed it hungrily.

'Yeah, it's all part of Lotta's brilliant plan so you couldn't make me tell you where the harp string was.' Whetstone edged closer, hoping he could reach the sword and shield. He had to get Lotta out of this cage and then both of them out of Jotunheim. Somehow. Whetstone wiped his sweaty hands down his trousers trying to think – Rhett the Bone-Breaker would probably do this sort of thing all the time.

'How – creative of you,' Loki purred. 'I'm curious, what was your plan if Lotta got captured and, I don't know, locked in a cage by the Giants?' Loki prowled closer; Whetstone hesitated. 'What's to stop *her* from telling me everything I want to know?'

Despite the ropes still pinning her arms to her sides, Lotta stuck her nose in the air. 'I'm not telling you anything. I've had interrogation training from Freyja – I'm impossible to crack.'

Flee let out a snort.

'I'm like a stone, a mountain. You'll get nothing from me,' Lotta continued.

'Are you sure?' Loki gestured at the cage. 'You are weaponless and alone. Except for a boy who didn't even notice you had been swapped for someone else.'

'I noticed,' Whetstone protested. His face growing hot, he snatched up the helmet and stuck it on his head to hide his blushes.

'Come on, Lotta,' Loki crooned, his voice soft. 'Stop pretending to be something you're not. You're not brave or strong enough to stand up against Glinting-Fire. But if you tell me where the last harp string is, I can protect you.'

Lotta barked a laugh.

'I'll tell Glinting-Fire you were helping me all along, that we were working together against this –' he gestured to Whetstone – 'worthless lump. He's no Hero, even with that stupid helmet.'

Whetstone took a step forward, about to protest, when a muffled rumbling followed by a crash echoed up the stone corridor. Everyone's eyes swivelled towards the sound.

'What was that?' Whetstone asked.

'Skrymir sounds unhappy,' Loki commented. 'He's not a

big fan of Heroes, either.' Pausing by the discarded sword and shield, Loki turned his attention back to the trainee Valkyrie. 'Don't make me use your shield against you, Lotta.'

Lotta sucked in a breath; her face took on a greenish tinge in the candlelight. Whetstone could feel his pulse racing; he couldn't risk Loki using his magic on Lotta.

'It won't work.' Lotta stuck her nose in the air, but her voice trembled.

'You've seen what I can do. The Valkyries are helpless against my magic.' Loki picked up the circular shield so that it balanced on one edge. 'It wouldn't take much to encourage you to be more talkative.' Green tendrils of creeping ice appeared on the shield, the magic snaking away from Loki's fingertips. 'Freyja's not here to save you now.'

Whetstone edged towards the man, looking for an opportunity to grab the shield. Rhett the Bone-Breaker was a Hero, a Champion of Valhalla. He could definitely save Lotta. Probably at the last second in a blaze of glory.

'Stop it,' Lotta muttered, her teeth clenched together. 'I'm not helping you.' Her body shook with the effort of resisting the magic. '*I am a stone,*' she recited. '*A mountain.*'

Flay and Flee ducked as more crashes echoed up from the Giants' feast.

'I don't think that's Skrymir. We need to get out of here,' Flay muttered, tugging on the cage door. 'Stupid thing – why won't you open?!'

'Let's use the mirror-door,' Flee suggested, reaching for it.

'No! It's broken,' Flay snapped. 'You'll come out in pieces.'

'Where is the harp string, Lotta?' Loki purred, ignoring the sounds of chaos from outside, his eyes locked on the trembling Valkyrie. Whetstone rocked on his toes, waiting for his moment.

The ice on the shield grew thicker; Lotta's eyes took on a shade of green. 'It's – it's in . . .'

There was no time left. Desperate to break the spell before Lotta could finish her sentence, Whetstone threw himself towards the shield. Loki sent him flying with a blast of magic.

Lotta's eyes unfocused; her mouth moved, repeating a single word over and over. Flee put her ear to Lotta's mouth. 'She says, "Valhalla."'

'What? No!' Whetstone rolled to his feet, shoving the helmet off his head.

The cup hopped out from between the bars. 'Oh dear.' It dived back into Whetstone's bag.

Loki smirked. 'Now let's see what else we can make you do.' He tapped his fingers on the shield. Lotta stopped trembling as the magic grew stronger.

Another crash echoed through the room, making the rafters shake. Dust rained down on the people on the table. Loki's head and shoulders were covered in grey, making him look like he had aged fifty years in a second. The twins coughed and spluttered, still pushing and shoving at the cage door. The shield skittered away from Loki's grasp, breaking the connection before he could fully enchant Lotta. Whetstone scrambled after it, desperate to reach it first. It wasn't over yet; he could still get them out of that cage and be the Hero.

Lotta shook her head, her eyes clearing. 'Ah – Ah –' Grime coated Lotta's face; her nose scrunched up.

Whetstone recognized that look: she was going to sneeze – there was too much dust in the air. He pulled the shield over his head.

'ACHOOO!'

Feathers filled the air, their edges burning with a purple flame. The ropes finally fell away and Lotta sat up, rubbing life back into her arms. The smell of burning feathers made everyone wheeze and cough.

Whetstone scrubbed dust out of his eyes with his sleeve. He scrambled back to the cage, snatching up Lotta's sword on the way. The hilt tingled under his fingers – magic swords were perfect for Heroes. With a mighty heave, Whetstone swung the blade at the padlock. It bounced off without leaving a scratch.

A jolly voice echoed along the corridor:

> *Asgard! Asgard!*
> *Home of Gods and fun.*

'Thor's here,' Flay spluttered. 'Glinting-Fire was supposed to keep him busy!' She shoved Whetstone away from the padlock and yanked on it with all her strength. It still didn't move.

The voice continued:

> *Asgard! Asgard!*
> *Until the Frost Giants come!*

. . . followed by the sound of something being hit repeatedly with a hammer.

'Freyja must've sent him,' Lotta replied, wiggling out of the last of the ropes. Whetstone was relieved to see her eyes return to their normal brown as Loki's magic faded. 'Pass me my sword.'

The door to the room slammed open, making them all jump. The sword fell from Whetstone's shocked fingers. Thor stood silhouetted against the flickering lights, looking tiny in the enormous doorway. 'Loki!' he bellowed. 'Freyja said you came here without me. Couldn't resist some Frost Giant bashing, huh?'

Whetstone looked around in alarm. 'Where *is* Loki?' The handsome man was nowhere to be seen.

Flee leaned out of the cage, waving a pale arm. 'Help us! We're trapped!'

'Captured by Frost Giants, eh? Don't despair, I'll rescue you!' Thor announced, hefting his hammer.

'No, it's fine – Rhett the Bone-Breaker's here,' replied Whetstone, pulling back his sleeve and sticking his hand into the padlock's keyhole, feeling for moving parts. 'I've got it.'

'MJOLNIR SMASH!' Raising his arm over his shoulder, Thor hurled his magic hammer at the birdcage.

'Duck!' screamed Flay, throwing herself to the ground. Whetstone copied her, landing on his stomach. The hammer whizzed over their heads making a low thrumming sound. It smashed into the birdcage with a fountain of sparks.

Whetstone blinked the stars out of his eyes – there was now a massive hole in the golden bars. The boy lifted himself on one elbow. 'What—'

'Keep down!' Lotta yelled as the hammer turned in the air, zooming back to Thor's hand.

'Thank you,' called Flee, sitting up and shoving her plaits out of her face.

'No sweat. Saving damsels in distress is what Heroes do!'

Whetstone winced.

Apparently satisfied at a job well done, Thor sauntered back into the corridor calling, 'Loki? Leave some Giants for me to fight!'

Lotta climbed out of the smashed cage. 'Come on, we can still beat Loki back to Asgard.' She snatched up her shield and pulled it on to her arm. 'Unless you'd rather take Flay with you as she's a much-better-Lotta?' Lotta pouted, tugging the sword out from under the twins.

'I'm sorry, all right!' Whetstone wiped his face, smearing it with dust and grime. 'And forget Asgard. We need to go to my foster mother's before Loki can get the last harp string.'

Lotta sheathed her sword, avoiding his eyes. 'Yeah, I'm sorry.'

'No time for that now. Argh!'

Flee grabbed him round the leg. 'I thought you were a

Hero – why couldn't you get us out of that cage?'

'*There once was a boy named Whetstone – Who everyone thought was a moan,*' the cup began, its voice muffled from being inside the bag.

'Because he's not a *proper* Hero like Thor,' Flay sneered, the ends of her hair singed. 'And he never will be.'

'I could've done it,' Whetstone began.

'Leave him alone.' Lotta prised Flee's white fingers away. 'We need to get out of here before Thor demolishes the castle.'

Whetstone pushed down the doubts swirling inside him. He looked up at Lotta. 'To Midgard?'

'To Midgard.'

Chapter Ten

Making It Big

Leaving the ice, snow, and the sound of Castle Utgard being reduced to rubble behind them, Whetstone and Lotta flapped as birds through the branches of the world tree. Guilt bubbled in Lotta's stomach. Valhalla was a big place, she told herself. It might take Loki days to find the harp string, and Freyja would hopefully notice

MIDGARD
PLEASE LEAVE IT
AS YOU FOUND IT

what he was up to and stop him. Lost in her thoughts, she scarcely noticed the flat, wide world beneath them and nearly crashed into a sign hanging from a nearby branch.

Midgard: Please leave it as you found it.

Lotta's mind drifted to Glinting-Fire, wondering if she had started her plan for Midgard domination yet, and what that might mean for the Vikings who lived there. One thing was for certain: Glinting-Fire wouldn't be leaving Midgard as she found it. Then Lotta remembered Vali. Was he down there somewhere too? She hoped he had made it out of Asgard like he had wanted.

Following Whetstone's coppery falcon, Lotta looped lower. Midgard grew in size beneath them. The green and brown land separating into individual farms and villages. Boulders dotted across the landscape like the bones of some huge animal, the land itself rising into sharp peaks and deep valleys. Lotta looked around with interest – she had never been to this part of Midgard before. Winter had crept across the land, making the sun low and the shadows long.

The falcon dived – skimming a clump of pine trees, their fresh scent blooming into the air and stinging Lotta's beak – before flopping exhaustedly into a leafless tree. Lotta swooped down to join him.

With a *pop*, the falcon disappeared and a boy sprawled in its place. The frosty tree bent under him, unable to support his weight. Whetstone crashed through the branches, sending icicles and frozen twigs tumbling, until he finally smacked into a branch sturdy enough to hold him. He gasped as the bag containing his golden helmet and magic cup landed on his stomach, knocking all the breath out of his body.

Lotta fluttered down, landing on a thick branch before transforming back into her human form.

With a groan, Whetstone sat up, clutching the bag. 'I guess it would have been better to land on the ground first, before transforming?' He swung his legs around so he was straddling the branch and started picking twigs out of his hair.

'Back in a tree, just like old times,' Lotta muttered, remembering their fateful journey down Yggdrasil. 'Where are we?'

With fingers that he kept thinking of as wings, Whetstone parted the branches in front of him. 'Drott,' he muttered, taking in the familiar landscape of purple moors and the occasional random boulder. In the distance, perched on a low hill, was the village he had grown up in, but things had changed while he had been gone. Whetstone carefully shuffled along the branch for a better look.

The village was now ringed with a tall wooden fence. In front of that lay a ditch, and guarding the ditch was a double ring of wooden spikes, all pointing towards the village. It took a few moments for Whetstone to make sense of what he was seeing. The village looked prepared for a siege, but none of the defences pointed outward to stop anyone attacking. Instead, all the spikes pointed inward – to prevent anyone *leaving*.

Blood-red raven banners fluttered over the walls. Lotta leaned forward. 'Glinting-Fire has been here, then,' she muttered, taking in the fortifications. Sourness settled in her stomach. 'I knew she had big plans, but I didn't quite imagine – this.' A Valkyrie in gleaming armour marched around the outside of the walls on patrol. 'It's a prison.'

'Good thing we don't need to get in there, then.' Whetstone turned his attention to a group of buildings a little way outside of the village. A sprawling collection of stone, wood and mud: Dunhowlin', his foster mother's orphanage for abandoned wolf cubs, and the place Whetstone had called home for the last twelve years. He had hoped never to come back to this place and see his wolf-mad foster mother ever again. Smoke curled up from the central chimney. A matching flicker of anxiety twisted around Whetstone's chest. The Angry Bogey must be home.

'Are you OK?' Lotta asked softly.

Whetstone eyed the buildings warily. Cold fingers of dread crept over him, making goosebumps rise on his arms. The thought of having to walk over there and ask the Angry

Bogey for the harp string made him feel physically sick. 'I'm fine.'

Lotta hunched her shoulders and dropped her chin to her chest. 'I know you're mad at me. I didn't mean to tell Loki where the harp string was.'

Snapping out of his memories, Whetstone turned to look at her. Lotta's knees were drawn up to her chest, her arms wrapped around them. 'That wasn't your fault,' Whetstone spluttered. 'He turned you into a green-eyed zombie!'

'I thought I was being so clever by hiding the harp string, but it all went wrong.' Lotta huddled into a tighter ball. 'Even my special interrogation training couldn't stop him.'

'It was a good plan –' Whetstone rubbed his neck – 'and it nearly worked. No one could've guessed that Loki would get the Giants to trap you in a cage.'

Lotta rested her chin on her knees. 'Good thing Thor turned up, really. Otherwise, I might still be there.'

Now it was Whetstone's turn to curl into a ball. He turned away from Lotta. 'Yeah, thanks for reminding me.'

'What? You'd rather I was still in that cage?'

Whetstone picked miserably at the tree bark. 'No, obviously. It's just, I thought if I was a proper Hero rather than just me, I'd be able to beat the Giants. Now I'm back in Drott and I'm the same loser I was when I left.'

Lotta bit her lip, not knowing what to say.

In the silence, the cup wiggled out of the bag. 'Are we not a bird any more?' it asked with its ruby eyes tight shut.

'And what's that horrible smell?'

'It's the wolf kennels – they get a bit whiffy.'

The cup opened its eyes and hopped along the branch. 'Uh huh, and what are we going to do about *them*?'

'Them?' With a sinking feeling, Whetstone peered through the branches to the base of the tree. Lotta gazed past her feet and gasped. Whetstone sat back again, his eyes closed. 'Just when I thought it couldn't get worse.' He wiped a hand over his clammy face. 'How many of them are there, do you reckon?'

The cup squinted. 'Two, maybe. Or fifty. I'm better with words than numbers, really.'

A pack of wolves lay around the base of the tree. Their furry faces all pointing up curiously at Whetstone and Lotta. A large wolf who had a white streak running along her back growled, the others joining in until the air was filled with an ominous rumbling. Whetstone squeezed the branch, the tree bark feeling reassuringly rough beneath his fingers.

'I thought you used to live here – why don't they recognize you?' Lotta asked, eyeing the wolves.

'I think they do. They used to try and eat me then too.'

A loud croak broke into their conversation. Whetstone glanced up to see a large black raven perched above them in the tree, watching them with bright eyes. Whetstone flapped a hand at it. 'Go on, shoo! We've got enough problems.'

The raven inched closer.

'Oh no.' Lotta shuffled towards the tree trunk. She grinned at the raven. 'Hi, Akrid.'

The raven shifted on its branch, its black talons flexing.

'That's Akrid?' Whetstone scrunched up his face. 'I thought Valkyries were supposed to turn into swans?'

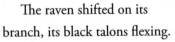

'We are.' Lotta gestured at the flags over the village. 'I guess Glinting-Fire must be using Loki's magic to change it to ravens.' The girl shifted on the branch. 'We need to go before Akrid tells Glinting-Fire we're here.'

Whetstone's skin prickled at the thought of returning to Dunhowlin'. 'Is your duck going to be able to fly faster than a raven?' he asked, stalling for time.

The cup jiggled. 'Despite being very intelligent birds,

ravens are surprisingly slow fliers, often overtaken by geese, wood pigeons and even the house sparrow.' Whetstone nodded. 'OK.'

He pulled the cloak around his shoulders, wishing it could turn him invisible or make him impervious to wolf bites.

'Head for the longhouse, the one with the blue door.'

'It was nice knowing you.' The cup shrugged. 'I'll tell your story after you've both been ripped to shreds.'

'You'll be ripped to shreds too – you're coming with us.' Whetstone tucked the protesting cup back into his bag with the helmet. He tried to block out the cup's scratchy voice and

concentrate. He just had to make it to the house, get inside and slam the door before anyone ate him or Lotta. Then he could worry about Angrboda. Whetstone shuffled as far along the branch as he could, stopping when he could feel it starting to bend.

The branch next to him wobbled as Lotta tucked her feet under herself, balancing on her toes. 'One . . .' she began. 'Two . . .'

'Three!' Whetstone yelled. He closed his eyes, threw out his arms and, with a flash of gold, transformed into the falcon. Below him, the wolves started to howl.

Whetstone dived off the branch. The wolf with the white streak snapped at him, making Whetstone roll through the air. Once away from the wolves, he spread his wings, swooping upward past Lotta flapping furiously as a grey-white duck. Out of the corner of his eye, Whetstone could see the raven following them. It was twice his size with dark ragged wings, but the falcon and duck were both faster.

He dived through the air, now only inches above the ground, his talons stretching out for the blue door of his foster mother's house. A waiting wolf lunged for him, catching his tail and sending him tumbling. With a *pop* and a flash of gold, Whetstone turned back into a boy. He landed badly, performing a sort of forward roll through the blue door and into the house. Lotta plunged in after him in a cloud of feathers.

Heart thumping, Whetstone shot out a leg, kicking the door closed behind them. The wolf threw itself against the door with a scrabble of claws.

'Hello, Whetstone.'

Whetstone rolled to his feet, his knees trembling. That voice haunted his nightmares. Watching him was a tall, bony woman wearing a dark red woollen dress decorated with clumps of wolf fur. Her black hair was scraped into a long plait, which coiled around her shoulders like a snake. She screwed up her pointy nose as though an unpleasant smell had wafted underneath.

'Yes, ma'am. Sorry, ma'am,' Whetstone began, his fingers instinctively pulling the cloak in around him. He felt his shoulders rise up around his ears. He tried to tell himself that he had faced down worse things: dragons, giant wolves, Freyja on a bad-hair day . . .

'I knew you'd come back.' The woman crossed her arms. 'You've got nowhere else to go.'

Whetstone felt sweat break out across his back. It was

all too easy to imagine Loki and the Angry Bogey working together. They were as mean and unpleasant as each other. His eyes raked the room, looking for clues to Loki's presence. Hopefully he hadn't made it to Drott yet. Beside him, Lotta got to her feet, groaning. She rubbed her shoulder where she had crash-landed.

Angrboda peered down her nose at the trainee Valkyrie. 'Who's this scum you've brought with you?'

Lotta pulled herself to her full height, matching Angrboda sneer for sneer. She put her hands on her hips. 'The only scum here is you.'

Whetstone stepped between them, his hands outstretched. 'You've got something of mine, a – silver string. I need it back. Then we'll go.'

The woman's dark eyes flashed. 'This is the thanks I get for all those years of looking after you.' Angrboda took a step forward; Whetstone tried not to flinch. The cup poked out of its bag to watch. 'You ungrateful brat, why would I want anything of yours? You came here with nothing, you left with nothing and you're still worth nothing.'

The cup gave a wiggle. 'Is this her?'

Whetstone nodded.

'I can't imagine why you left.'

Angrboda bared her horsey teeth.

'Are you sure she's got the harp string?' The cup nodded at Angrboda. 'Cos if you could choose how you looked, why would you want to look like that?'

130

Angrboda started to laugh, a rich dark sound, which filled the corners of the room. She hadn't laughed much when Whetstone lived there, usually only when something unpleasant was about to happen to him. Lotta's eyebrows scrunched together in confusion. Whetstone took a step back, clutching the bag to his chest.

In front of his eyes, the woman started to grow. Her body stretching upward as if someone had reached down and grabbed her head while leaving her feet stuck to the floor. Whetstone stumbled further back in shock.

The cup goggled. 'What's happening? Why is she so tall?'

Angrboda shook her head, masses of long dark hair coming loose from her plait. Fine strands drifted around her head like a gauzy curtain. Still laughing, the woman started to swell, her body filling out to keep her in proportion with her height. Whetstone was relieved to see that her clothes were growing with her.

There once was a woman named Angr,

the cup improvised

> *Who hid on Midgard, what a clanger!*
> *She's got really tall,*
> *That's not weird at all,*
> *And no one would think to thank her.*

Angrboda's head brushed against the ceiling as Lotta fumbled with the door and Whetstone stood stunned. The woman was forced to crouch down as she continued to grow. Her face changed, softening from its sharp lines into something younger. Her skin started to take on a bluish tone.

'She's a Frost Giant!' the cup squeaked, diving back into the bag.

Pulling open the door, Lotta shoved Whetstone outside and they staggered away. Lotta produced her sword. Wolves prowled to and fro, not wanting to get too close to the shuddering building or silvery blade.

The boy stood staring at the house as it twisted and shook. Whetstone hated Angrboda, but he had never imagined that she might be anything other than human.

Lotta grabbed hold of his sleeve, trying to hustle him further away. 'Snap out of it, Whetstone, or we'll be squished!'

With a splintering sound, the timbers that made up the house started to bend and break as Angrboda continued to grow. The wolves howled, their attention focused on the house, which trembled as if it were an enormous egg with a chick trying to hatch out of it.

Lotta lifted her shield as, with a final *crack*, Angrboda's house collapsed to the ground. Coughing and waving away the dust, Whetstone found himself staring at an enormous swirl of red skirts. His gaze travelled up, and up, and up, until it reached a blue-skinned face topped with long purple hair.

Angrboda was so big, the buildings around her barely came up to her knees. Whetstone had only seen people that size in Jotunheim. He swayed slightly. Something glinted around one of her fingers. 'She's wearing the harp string,' he gasped, pointing.

'Brilliant – how do we get it?' Lotta shook dust out of her hair. 'Have you got a plan?'

Whetstone wiped his sleeve over his face. 'Surprisingly, no.'

Chapter Eleven

A Giant Problem

With a giggle that made boulders wobble, Angrboda lifted a foot the size of a wagon, thumping it down at where Whetstone and Lotta stood.

'Move!' Lotta sprinted along a narrow muddy track.

'Head for the kennels,' Whetstone panted, following her. 'She won't stand on them in case she hurts the wolves.'

High above them, Angrboda giggled again. She lifted her foot and stamped back down, crunching through fences and sending wolves scattering.

'You were saying?' Lotta threw herself behind a narrow wooden building. In a flurry of black feathers, a raven took off from the roof, croaking loudly. 'Not you again,' Lotta muttered, pulling her helmet low over her eyes. Whetstone slammed into the wall beside her, breathing hard.

Angrboda's face loomed over them, blotting out the winter sunlight. Whetstone and Lotta flinched away. With a smile that showed off teeth the size of tombstones, the Giant reached down and picked up Whetstone, pinching the feathered cloak between her thumb and forefinger.

Whetstone's stomach dropped as he was lifted high into the air. He grabbed at the cloak to stop it choking him, and also to stop himself from slipping free and falling. The bag with the cup and helmet lay abandoned on the ground. Far below, Lotta yelled and waved her sword.

Angrboda held the boy up to her eye; Whetstone felt he could almost fall into those endless dark pits. No one looked good with their face that big: Angrboda's nostrils were the size of Whetstone's hand, each pore and pockmark clearly visible. She glanced down at something at her feet and, with a kick, sent Lotta flying, sword and shield still in her hands. The trainee Valkyrie landed with a grunt in a clump of stubby trees.

Angrboda focused on Whetstone. She rolled her shoulders. 'It feels good to be back at my true size,' she said in a voice that could shake mountains. 'I never did like being so small.'

Whetstone swung, helpless and terrified, in the air. 'You don't have to do this,' he panted, clinging on to the cloak. 'Just give me the harp string and I can stop Loki.'

The Frost Giant laughed. 'But I want to do it. This day has been a long time coming, Whetstone.' She flicked the boy into the air before catching him in an enormous fist. 'The Gods deserve it for what they did to my children.'

'You mean the wolves?' His arms pinned to his sides, Whetstone felt the air being slowly squeezed out of his lungs. 'They look OK to me.' Lack of oxygen made dark spots dance in front of the boy's eyes. He focused on the silvery harp string still wrapped around Angrboda's finger like a ring.

The Giant snorted. 'No, my real children. I believe you've

136

already met them – Jormungandr, Hel and Fenrir.'

Whetstone's body went completely rigid in shock. The world seemed to tilt around him. Jormungandr was a monstrous sea serpent who had smashed apart a longboat in an attempt to eat him. Hel, the half-skeleton Queen of the Dead, ruled Helheim, where his father was a prisoner. And Fenrir was a gigantic wolf who – well, who just wanted his tummy tickled.

Angrboda continued, 'Odin separated us across the Nine Worlds – he was worried we were dangerous.' She barked a laugh, her sour breath wafting over Whetstone. 'But soon my family will be together again.' Her hair swung against her face in a way that reminded Whetstone of Hel.

'You can't,' Whetstone panted, breathless. He wiggled, trying to reach the harp string. 'Loki will destroy everything.'

Angrboda's face loomed closer. 'Maybe everything deserves to be destroyed. Then we can start again.'

Behind her head, colours twinkled in the sky: the Bifrost Bridge, which linked Asgard and Midgard in the form of a rainbow. Whetstone's stomach clenched; Loki must've found the second harp string. He had to stop him from reaching Angrboda and getting the third. The boy fixed his eyes on his foster mother's enormous ones. 'Please, Angrboda. That harp string isn't yours. Please give it back to me.'

Angrboda tilted her head, her dark purple hair moving in the breeze, but before she could reply, there was a sense of frantic movement and a frenzied quacking. A shape like a feathered arrow dived through the air.

'Lotta!' Whetstone gasped.

Angrboda stepped back in surprise as Duck-Lotta plunged towards her face. Then Whetstone realized Lotta wasn't alone. A cloud of ravens swooped after her. Angrboda threw up an enormous hand to block them and the ravens scattered. In her other hand, her grip around Whetstone loosened and the boy slipped, plunging towards the ground below.

Whetstone flailed, desperately trying to find the edge of the cloak so he could transform before he hit anything solid.

With a heavy thud, Whetstone slammed into something warm and sweaty. Brown hair filled his vision and the scent of horses made him want to sneeze. Whetstone fumbled for something to grab on to. He had landed across the back of a horse. A horse in mid-air.

'What are you doing? Get off Thunder Trumper!'

Trying not to slip as the horse trotted through the sky, Whetstone glanced up to see a girl with one silver plait and one singed tuft. She screwed her face into a snooty expression.

'Flay?' he gasped. The twins must've escaped Jotunheim.

Angrboda's laughter reverberated as she reached forward, trying to snatch him off the back of the horse.

'Get me out of here!' Whetstone

grabbed hold of Flay to stop himself falling.

'No way.' The girl thrust one hand into his face. 'Flee – some help here!'

Flee pranced past, her horse trotting like it was taking part in a private dressage contest.

Whetstone stretched past Flay, reaching the reins. Feathers filled the air as Lotta and the Valkyries swooped around them, performing a twisting loop-the-loop around the horse. Despite everything, Whetstone was impressed. The cup was right – ducks really were faster than ravens.

In an explosion of feathers, Lotta landed on the horse, wedging herself in between Flay and Whetstone and transforming back into her human form. 'Go!' she shrieked, digging her boots into the horse's sides. The horse reared and tossed his mane, protesting at the extra passengers.

'Will all of you GET OFF!' Flay fought to keep control of the horse, who cantered sideways through the air.

Darkness loomed as Angrboda made another grab for them.

'She's got the harp string around her finger,' Whetstone gasped, trying not to be sick.

Snatching up her sword and nearly sending Whetstone tumbling, Lotta reached out, managing to catch the silvery harp string with her blade. The harp string came loose and slipped away from a surprised Angrboda.

Whetstone lunged sideways, trying to snatch it as it fell. His fingers closed around the string, but it slid out of his sweaty hands. 'Down!' he yelled. Flay's horse thrashed its hooves, colliding with Flee.

The world became a confusion of whirling images, horsehair, armour and the sound of someone screaming. Whetstone thought it might be him. He closed his eyes and held on tightly to Lotta, who was gripping on to Flay. The horse righted itself and Whetstone forced open his eyes. The harp string glinted in the winter sunshine. It drifted sideways in the breeze, before dropping straight into the waiting hands of a man with golden hair and a red tunic.

'Loki!' Lotta spat.

With a *whoompf* and a scattering of ravens, Loki swelled in size to stand beside Angrboda. Unlike Angrboda, with her blue skin, he looked exactly as he had before, but now he was the height of a mountain.

Flay's horse whinnied and bucked in surprise, making all three of its passengers yelp and cling on tighter.

The Fire Giant dangled the harp string between his fingers; it looked like a tiny silver thread in his hands. 'Thank you, Whetstone,' he boomed, his voice echoing across the landscape.

'No!' Whetstone bellowed.

With a cold laugh, Loki started to shrink again, growing smaller and smaller but staying hovering in mid-air so he remained level with Angrboda's head.

'Damn Sky-Walking Shoes,' Lotta muttered through gritted teeth as the man gave them a jaunty wave and turned in the air to walk away. Angrboda blew him a kiss.

'There's still a chance!' Whetstone shouted. 'We have to stop him before he can reach the harp frame!'

Lotta nodded and, with a loud *crack*, transformed back

into a duck.
She leaped off
the horse's back
and into the sky,
plunging downward
while
flapping furiously.

Whetstone spread out his arms
and, in a flash of gold, transformed
into the falcon. Flay's horse bucked,
startled at the magic that was happening
behind its ears. Flay was forced to cling on
around its neck.

'Byeeee!' called Flee.

Soaring through the air, Whetstone fixed his eyes on the tiny
figure of Loki making his way through the sky. Rainbow lights
twinkled around him as he summoned down the Bifrost Bridge.

A bedraggled duck appeared beside Whetstone, feathers in
different shades of grey and white stuck out in all directions. She
quacked and flapped her wings, fighting for height as behind her
more ravens shot into the sky like dark arrows. The Valkyrie birds
surrounded Lotta, mobbing her, pecking with their sharp beaks.

Lotta squawked, twisting to try and fend them off.
Whetstone the Falcon circled, gaining height before turning

back and folding his wings in a dive, plunging down towards the swarming Valkyries.

The birds scattered. Whetstone flattened his wings trying to stop before he ended up back in Drott. Behind him he heard a loud *crack* and Lotta transformed into her human form but now with large wings sticking out of her back. She aimed a kick at an approaching raven, who was forced to spiral away to avoid being hurt. Lotta thrashed her large wings, creating a draught which sent the rest of the birds tumbling. Whetstone fought to avoid being knocked out of the sky.

'Get on to the rainbow bridge,' Lotta shouted, pointing. 'Come on, we can still catch him.' She turned in mid-air, diving through the shining lights and leaving only ripples behind her.

Closing his eyes, Whetstone crashed through the rainbow wall – lights hit his skin like sharp pin pricks of hail. The shock made him transform back into a human. His feet slipped and he fell, gasping, on to the floor of a smooth rainbow-coloured tunnel.

Lotta yanked him to his feet, her dark skin covered in strange patterns from the lights. 'No time for lying about!' She set off at a jog, heading up the tunnel.

Whetstone ran a sleeve over his hair, which was crackling with static. Through the rainbow walls he could see Valkyries circling, unsure of whether to follow them or to stay in Drott. Whetstone gulped and scrabbled after Lotta, his feet making the rainbow ring hollowly.

The branches of Yggdrasil appeared above them, hazy through the rainbow lights. The sky-roof of Midgard was almost in reach. They were nearly there.

Chapter Twelve

Skera Harp

Indifferent to the children following him, Loki stepped out of the Bifrost Bridge and into the branches of Yggdrasil. Unwrapping the last harp string from around his fingers, the Trickster scooped up the golden harp from its hiding place. The words *Skera: I cut* were engraved deeply into the wooden frame topped by a carved dragon's head like those found on longboats. Just like a longboat, the harp could lead the owner into strange new worlds. Created by the Dwarves as a way of travelling between the Nine Worlds, the magic harp had been stolen by Loki to achieve his own evil ends.

Humming gently to himself, the man held the third string to the light before threading it through the harp. Two silver stings already glittered in place. Loki tightened the pegs, power thrumming through the harp ready to dance at the Trickster's fingertips.

Loki hadn't been idle while searching for the strings. He had also uncovered as much as he could of the magic that controlled the harp – how it worked and how to manipulate it. Each of the strings might contain their own magic, but when played together, they were even more powerful. Play the strings in a certain order and the walls between different worlds opened like petals on a flower. Play the strings in another way and the walls became as solid as a locked door. Loki smiled his twisted smile and flexed his fingers, ready to play.

Chapter Thirteen

Worlds Collide

The world – shifted.

The sky-roof above Midgard rang like an enormous gong, sending ripples along the rainbow bridge. Whetstone stumbled, falling to his knees. Ahead of him, Lotta slipped as her boots wobbled out from under her.

A series of musical notes, just on the edge of hearing, filled the air with static, making Whetstone's skin prickle. The boy looked up in confusion. 'Was that . . . ?'

Lotta nodded, her jaw tight. 'I think so.' She pulled herself upright.

The sky flickered. Different skies appeared and vanished in the blink of an eye. Boiling grey clouds, then open blue. The endless red horizon of Helheim gave way to the snow-filled skies of Jotunheim. Whetstone gulped and stared at his feet, the changing skies making him feel queasy. This, however, was a mistake as the land beneath him was no better, seething and shifting as different worlds all fought to exist in the same place at the same time. Mountain ranges, open plains, lush forests and Viking villages flashed into view before being replaced by something else.

Lotta skidded back towards him. 'The worlds are colliding!' she yelled. 'Loki has brought them all here.' As she spoke, the rainbow lights started to flash and fade, leaving stars trailing across Whetstone's vision. 'The bridge won't exist much longer.' Lotta stumbled, her arm passing through the tunnel's wall. 'It's only supposed to link Midgard and Asgard – not whatever *this* is!'

Whetstone fumbled for the edges of the falcon cloak. 'Let's

go,' he began, before swirling tentacles of grey fog submerged him.

'Mists from Niflheim –' Lotta coughed, from somewhere in the murk. 'That means—'

A flash of red scales and breath that smelt like sulphur washed over them.

'Nidhogg!' Whetstone spluttered.

Nidhogg was the dragon who lived in the lowest and

darkest of the Nine Worlds, where he watched over the spirits of the unworthy dead.

Whetstone goggled as a dark shape with wings the size of boats swooped past. 'We can't fly out there – we'll be toast!'

'What else do you suggest?' came Lotta's voice.

The bridge gave another shudder, sending them both skidding backwards. They emerged out of the mists gasping and spluttering. With a final jolt, the rainbow vanished, flicking them out into the ever-changing sky.

'Argh!' The world spun around Whetstone, his stomach feeling as if it had been left behind on the bridge. His vision turned blue as an enormous hand closed around him, plucking him out of the air. Whetstone shoved at the hand and panted as the breath was squeezed out of his lungs. He stared up, expecting to see Angrboda's gigantic face peering down smugly at him. Instead, a much younger face swam into focus.

'Dollies!'

'Gert?' Whetstone gasped.

The girl grinned. Her white eyelashes standing out clearly against her blue face. She lifted her other hand in which was held –

'Lotta!'

'Put me down!' The trainee Valkyrie wiggled in the Giant girl's grip, her hands pummelling the girl's fingers.

'Mummy says I can have a real doll's house here,' the girl said. 'You can live in it if you like.'

'No thanks,' Whetstone sputtered.

'What have you got there, Gert?' With a rustle of skirts, a

purple-haired Frost Giant peered down at them. She wrinkled up her nose in disgust. 'Urgh. Put them down – you don't know where they've been.'

'But –' Gert protested.

'We'll get you some cleaner-looking ones after we've seen Auntie Angrboda,' the Giant woman continued, prising Gert's hand open and shaking Whetstone free. The boy tumbled to the ground, thankfully landing in a large snowdrift, which had just popped into being. Lotta fell down next to him as, complaining, Gert was led away.

Whetstone wiped snow off his face and immediately rolled out of the way as a group of Vikings sprinted past trying to avoid Nidhogg, who was using them as target practice. Lotta sat up, shaking snowflakes out of her black curls. Whetstone helped her to her feet and they tucked themselves behind a nearby boulder.

Down on the ground, things were even worse than up in the air. The land rose and fell. One moment they were in a snowdrift; the next knee-deep in flowers. Hysterical Vikings flooded out of Drott, trying to escape the Giants, dragon and other creatures which had seemingly appeared out of thin air.

Whetstone dug his fingers into the boulder. 'I thought Loki was going to open the walls between worlds – I didn't think he was going to bring all the worlds here!'

Lotta shook her head. 'It gets worse. Where are the Gods? If the worlds are colliding, why haven't they appeared?'

Whetstone stared around in amazement; she was right.

'I can see Midgard. The mist must be Niflheim. The Giants are from Jotunheim.'

With the chatter of angry sparrows, a crowd of tiny silvery creatures landed on the boulder they were sheltering behind.

'Elves!' Lotta dragged Whetstone away. 'From Alfheim!'

'Why are we running?' Whetstone panted. 'What can Elves do?'

Behind them came a screech, and a cloud of tiny arrows filled the air. Vikings fell where they stood as the arrows struck them.

'That,' Lotta gasped. 'Elf-shot. Don't let their arrows touch you.' A wave of heat blasted over them as the world changed again. Volcanos spitting red and green sparks surged up out of the ground, dissolving the snow. 'Muspell,' Lotta explained as the

ground danced beneath their feet. 'Fire Giants.' The Frost Giants roared in protest and, high above, the dragon Nidhogg looped the loop around a cloud of ash.

Pushing their way into a so-far-untouched clump of trees, Lotta peered out at the unfolding chaos. 'Loki must've found a way

of only opening *some* of the walls between worlds. That's why there's no Asgard or Vanaheim.' She looked around carefully. 'No Svartalfheim either, because bringing the Dwarves here would be too convenient.'

Whetstone nodded. 'You know who else we're missing? Hel.'

'Not for long.' Lotta raised a trembling finger as sticky black-tar-like strands seethed out of the gritty Muspell soil. 'It's the Helhest!'

The Helhest was Hel's magical servant, able to change shape and become anything she needed it to. The strands rose, sticking upward like the fingers of an enormous hand. The shape twisted, curving into a towering archway decorated with images of bones and laughing skulls. Darkness poured out of the arch like a flowing river, sizzling as it came into contact with the other worlds around it.

Whetstone gasped. 'I hope Vali's not here to see this. He'll be wishing he'd stayed in Asgard!'

'Duck!' Lotta screamed as the world was suddenly filled with grey fur. A wolf the size of a building bounded out of the Helhest archway and over their heads, paws like cartwheels crushing flowers and thumping into snowdrifts. 'It's Fenrir!'

The wolf shook snowflakes and ash out of his coat. Vikings screamed at the sight of his gaping jaws and blood-red tongue. 'He's got bigger.' Whetstone pushed himself up on his elbows. The wolf sniffed the air and bounded away, heading towards the group of Frost Giants who had clustered around Angrboda. He jumped up at his mother, leaving massive muddy pawprints over her woollen dress.

'My furry baby!' Angrboda cooed.

Then Hel herself appeared. Half living girl, half skeleton, and all entitled brat. The Queen of the Dead was borne forward on a mighty boat made of toenails, floating on the river of darkness.

'How did she get Naglfar?' Whetstone gasped, peering out between what was left of the trees. 'I thought Loki had that.'

'Seriously, that's your question?' Lotta elbowed him.

'We're all going to die!' shrieked a passing Viking who Whetstone recognized as Olaf the Sweaty, blacksmith of Drott.

'I find that offensive,' snapped the spirit of a long-dead Viking from Niflheim, drifting past. 'Some of us are already dead.'

'You can't call us *dead* – that's so cringe,' argued another spirit, rolling her eyes.

But Whetstone wasn't paying any attention to them. His eyes were fixed on another figure who had appeared out of the archway.

'Dad?'

Thinner than he had last seen him in Helheim but otherwise apparently unharmed – although his nose now had a distinct kink where Whetstone had accidentally broken it – stood Whetstone's father. Whetstone felt the blood fizz in his veins.

Lotta grabbed Whetstone's arm, holding him down before he could gain the attention of the stocky man with a long beard and patched clothes.

'He's still alive!' Whetstone tried to wrestle himself free. 'Let go!'

'You cannot be serious!' Lotta hissed. She dragged Whetstone towards a small stone building which had so far avoided being trampled or burned to the ground. Through his confusion, Whetstone recognized it as having been once used to stockpile onions. 'Can you imagine what Hel would do to us if she knew we were here? We don't have Freyja to help us this time!' Yanking the door open, she hustled him inside. 'We need – a plan.'

Whetstone goggled at her.

The light vanished as the door slammed shut. Whetstone shoved Lotta away, fumbling for the handle. Forget Lotta's concerns – he couldn't leave his dad out there like this.

A blade pressed to Whetstone's ribs. The boy felt his knees turn to jelly. His scrabbling fingers stilled. 'Are you friend or foe?' hissed a voice in his ear. Hair tickled his neck.

'Erm –' Whetstone could feel his heart hammering against his chest. He swivelled his eyes sideways trying to see who was threatening him. His eyes started to adjust to the gloom and a blur of white appeared beside him.

'I know you want to find your dad, but we can't, not right now,' said Lotta's voice in the darkness. 'He'll be fine for a bit longer.' Then after Whetstone didn't reply, she added, 'What is it? Are you sulking now?'

'No, but – we're not alone,' Whetstone squeaked as the blade pressed closer.

Lotta instinctively reached for her sword and raised her shield. Coloured lights shimmered, casting strange shadows around the stone room.

'Calm down,' said a voice from deep in the shadows. 'They're just kids.'

A woman with blonde hair and dressed in white moved past Whetstone towards Lotta. 'This one is in armour,' she said, giving Lotta a poke. 'Could be a Valkyrie spy.'

'She is a Valkyrie, but we're not spies.' Whetstone rubbed his side.

'I say we gut them now,' the woman continued. 'Just to be on the safe side.'

The other voice sighed. 'You can't gut everyone, Marta.'

'You say that, Grimnir –' Marta sniggered – 'but it would have saved a lot of trouble if I had simply gutted Loki when I met him.'

Whetstone wobbled. His stomach felt as if it had fallen into his boots. Beside him, Lotta gasped.

Across the room a candle flickered to life, filling the room with warm light. Whetstone found himself staring into a pale face he had regularly seen reflected back at him in the mirrors at Freyja's Great Hall. 'Mum?'

❋

On the edge of the candlelight, Whetstone sat on a wooden box next to his mother, not knowing quite what to say.

'I'm sorry for almost stabbing you,' the woman began. Her skin and hair as pale as moonlight, she almost glowed against the darkness. From outside came the muffled sound of screaming and panicked Vikings, but inside the stone hut the world was eerily calm.

'Occupational hazard,' Whetstone replied, more casually than he felt. 'I'm actually quite used to almost being stabbed.' Whetstone eyed the blade. 'That's the bit of broken mirror from the birdcage!'

'A souvenir from Loki,' Marta explained, twisting the jagged green glass in her hands. Strips of material had been wrapped around one end as a makeshift handle. 'Giant magic is pretty rare, so I thought I'd take it as payment for twelve years of golden tears.' A boom came from outside, making them all flinch. Marta raised the knife. 'Sorry, I'm just a bit jumpy at the moment.'

Whetstone nodded. 'Loki has that effect on people. You gave him the harp string.'

Marta sighed. 'It seemed like a good deal at the time.' She

tucked the knife into her belt. 'But Midgard is different to how I remember.'

'Midgard isn't usually like this. Loki has opened the walls between worlds.' A loud wolf howl echoed from outside, making the candle quiver. 'I think that was Fenrir – he's not usually here either.' Twisting the falcon cloak between his fingers, Whetstone added, 'I saw Dad.'

His mum gripped his arm. 'Hod? He's still alive?'

Whetstone stared at her hand on his arm, her fingers white in the gloom. 'He's here, with Hel. I tried, but I couldn't get him out of Helheim.'

'If he's still alive, then there's still hope.' Marta released his arm. 'I'm sure you did your best.'

Whetstone nodded miserably.

'What's it like being a Hero, then?'

Whetstone shrugged. 'I don't think I'm very good at it. After I couldn't save Dad, I tried to be more like Thor and the other Vikings in Valhalla –' he gave a snort – 'I even fought a man named Stinky Stein in single combat to prove I was a real Hero. But everything went a bit wrong. I even lost my Hero helmet.'

'This helmet?' asked Grimnir, a man with a white beard and the only other grown-up in the stone room. He produced a cloth bag from beside him and passed it to Whetstone.

'How did you get that?'

Something wiggled inside the bag, and the cup hopped on to Whetstone's hand. 'There you are. You will not *believe* what has happened.'

157

'I think I might,' said Whetstone with a small smile.

'What on Midgard is that?' His mother leaned closer. The cup jumped on to her palm.

'It's a magical talking cup,' Whetstone explained. 'It can tell the future, although it mostly just does annoying riddles.'

The cup blew a loud raspberry. From outside the hut came the crackling of fires and a blast of sulphuric smoke.

'So now you've got your helmet back, what are you going to do next?' Marta coughed, passing the cup back to Whetstone. 'Something – bold?'

'What's the point?' Whetstone shrugged, the golden helmet glinting up at him from inside the bag. 'I tried being a Hero, I tried being me, and none of it worked. Loki still got the harp strings. We're probably safer staying put and living in this hovel forever.'

'Get over yourself.' Lotta sniffed. 'What we need is a *plan*.'

Whetstone groaned. 'Not another one. They haven't worked out that well so far.'

'Shh. I'm thinking.' Lotta paced back and forth in the narrow space, listing on her fingers. 'First, we need to get out of here without being crushed, burned, shot by Elves or eaten. Also avoiding the Valkyries, who are being mind-controlled by Glinting-Fire—'

'Is she the short bossy one with the tattoos?' interrupted Grimnir.

'That's her.'

The man nodded. 'That's who broke into Drott and put up the big spiky fence.'

158

'Didn't anyone try to stop her?' asked Whetstone.

'It was the midwinter feast.' Grimnir tapped his walking stick on the ground. 'We were all in the Great Hall celebrating when they arrived. No one put up a fight – we thought the Valkyries would take us up to eternal feasting in Valhalla, not make us prisoners inside our village.'

Whetstone nodded. 'Makes sense.'

Their heads turned towards scrabbling noises at the door. Silvery fingers appeared in the cracks.

'More Elves,' Marta huffed, leaning on the door to keep it closed. 'They were the ones who chased us in here in the first place.'

'After that,' Lotta continued, ignoring the Elves, 'we need to find Loki, track down wherever he has hidden the magic harp, get it away from him, figure out how to play it, separate the Nine Worlds again –' Lotta sucked in breath – 'and make our way to Svartalfheim to return the harp to the Dwarves, breaking the curse and fixing everything.'

'When you say it like that, it sounds easy.' Whetstone sighed.

'How are you going to do it?' asked Grimnir.

Lotta threw her arms in the air. 'I have no idea.' She sat down with a thump next to Whetstone. 'This is impossible.' She rested her head in her hands with a sigh.

After a few awkward seconds, Whetstone gave her a nudge. 'Don't say that. You're the one who's always telling me not to give up.'

'Well, I was wrong,' Lotta muttered without looking at

him. 'We couldn't have made things worse if we'd tried.'

Whetstone shuffled his feet. It wasn't like Lotta to just give in. 'Come on, there must be something we can do.'

'Like what? Go out there and fight all the Giants and monsters? Fine. After you,' Lotta replied indistinctly.

'You must have some ideas,' Whetstone said encouragingly. 'You're always coming up with plans.'

'Rubbish plans.'

Whetstone glanced at Marta and Grimnir, both of whom looked away. Whetstone pulled at the collar of his shirt. 'Lotta, there's no way I would have made it this far without you. Please, I can't do this by myself.'

'You're the one who wanted to live here in this stinky shed forever,' Lotta pointed out.

'Yeah, but – I thought you would try to talk me out of it. You usually do.'

Lotta gave a snort. 'Maybe *I* should try being a Hero for a change.'

Whetstone winced. 'I don't think that would help.'

'I think you would do well to remember the skills that you already have,' Grimnir suggested, resting his hands on top of his staff. 'You're stronger than you think.'

Whetstone squinted at him. 'How do you know what skills we have?'

The man shrugged. 'You're obviously resourceful young people to have made it this far.'

Whetstone peered closer at the man. 'Have we met before? You look sort of familiar.'

Before the man could answer, a magically loud voice echoed around the stone hut.

'Citizens of Midgard –'

The sounds of screaming and crying quietened.

'Fear not. I and the Valkyries are here to save you!'

Lotta's head shot up. Shoving Marta aside, she tugged the door open and dashed out.

'Who was that?' Marta asked, helping Grimnir to his feet. Whetstone shrugged and they followed Lotta outside.

The volcanos had vanished, replaced by endless snowfields. The sky above them was blank, grey and still, like the inside of an egg. Whetstone shivered into his cloak. He glanced around. The stone building was the only thing left standing, the clump of trees it had stood beside now turned to toothpicks.

Grimnir raised his staff to point at a spot of darkness in the sky. 'Look.'

Lotta stood a few feet away, staring upward. Even the Vikings of Drott had stopped running around, turning instead to watch as the dark shape grew larger.

'What is it?' Whetstone hissed, shading his eyes and moving to stand next to Lotta.

Lotta glanced at him, her eyes wide. The dark shape formed into a woman on a flying horse.

Clutching a megaphone, Glinting-Fire descended, her thick black plaits flicked up by the wind, her armour a gleaming blue. Around her hung a thundercloud of ravens. The Vikings all stood and stared agog at this new vision; even some of the Giants were watching. Nidhogg hung in the sky

like a giant bat, flapping his wings slowly, waiting to see what would happen next.

Glinting-Fire raised the megaphone. 'Return to the village square and we will take care of you.'

The Vikings goggled. 'I know you,' one shouted, raising a meaty finger to point at her. 'You're the one who messed up our village.'

'We have built you defences,' Glinting-Fire corrected, her horse beating his wings to stay aloft. 'You should be thanking us. We alone stand between you and utter destruction.'

At this moment, as if waiting for his cue, an enormous sea serpent reared up, towering over the Vikings of Drott. His snakelike body was thicker than a house, four horns decorated a terrifying head, which looked half lizard, half bull.

'It's the Midgard Serpent!' squeaked a woman whose face

had turned white with fear. 'We're not even anywhere near the coast!'

'Jorm-y!' bellowed Angrboda, rushing towards him, her feet flattening anyone or anything unlucky enough to get in her way. 'Come to Mummy!' The massive wolf, Fenrir, bounded along behind her.

The Vikings gasped in horror and started flooding back towards the centre of the village. With bursts of dark feathers, the ravens turned back into Valkyries. Lining the route, they formed a barrier between the Vikings and the Giants, Elves and other magical creatures. Whetstone, Lotta, Marta and Grimnir were helpless against the tide of people sweeping them back to the 'safety' of the village.

Chapter Fourteen

Rise of the Valkyries

'What is Glinting-Fire up to?' Still clutching his cloth bag, Whetstone was bundled through the streets by the press of people. Behind him, Lotta stared at the Valkyries lining the route, now all dressed in blue armour like Glinting-Fire, their eyes still glassy-green from Loki's magic. Lotta pulled her helmet low over her face as she was hustled deeper into Drott. Marta bumped along, tripping over Lotta's heels.

This was not how Whetstone had hoped his homecoming to Drott would be. In his dreams, his arrival was accompanied by cheering, and all the people who had ever doubted or been mean to him were throwing flowers and asking for his autograph. He hadn't expected to be dragged in by a flood of panicking Vikings. He reached out to catch his mum's hand, his eyes flicking from side to side, taking in the familiar buildings.

Despite his rolling dread at what was happening, Whetstone couldn't help but look around in wonder. Drott seemed so much *smaller* than he'd remembered. On his right was the home of Tomaz the Terrible, which he shared with his brother, Barri, who raised small yappy dogs. Angrboda had a running feud with Barri as her wolves considered the small yappy dogs to be a snack. No yapping came from their house today, and no sparks came from Olaf the Sweaty's blacksmith's forge either.

Vikings poured into the village square, following Glinting-Fire. She sat astride her flying horse like a pea on a barrel, as she was quite small and the horse very large. The horse pranced in the air above the Great Hall. The doors hung open and Whetstone could just see the glint of something green inside.

Lotta waved to catch his attention. 'The Valkyrie shields,' she mouthed, pointing.

Vikings shoved their way into the square – every person who lived for miles around must be there. Whetstone found himself elbow to elbow with Pjorn the Pig Wrestler, who was being propped up by his friends as he still had a number of Elf arrows sticking out of his back. Behind him, Norm the Merciless breathed down Whetstone's neck. Whetstone's eyes raked over a hundred familiar faces as his mum squeezed his hand. Whetstone looked at her: her jaw was tight, her eyes focused on the hovering Valkyrie.

Glinting-Fire's horse strutted lower, aiming for a raised platform which had been built in front of the Great Hall. A semicircle of Valkyries waited there. Turning with difficulty to look behind him, Whetstone realized that the whole square was lined by Valkyries, all with glowing green eyes.

They were trapped. A shiver ran down his spine.

'People of Drott,' Glinting-Fire began as her horse landed

on the platform. 'You are in grave danger. The walls between the Nine Worlds have been opened. Midgard is no longer safe from the monsters.'

The Vikings murmured, their eyes fixed on the tiny Valkyrie Leader.

'Giants, Dragons, Elves, the unworthy dead. All are here,' Glinting-Fire continued. 'And where are your Gods to protect you? They have abandoned you in your hour of need. Too preoccupied with their own petty squabbles.'

In the skies over the village appeared a vision of Asgard. Whetstone gasped. He could clearly see Freyja in her cat dressing gown arguing with Frigg and Thor. Thor shrugged and tossed his hammer in the air before catching it one-handed. Frigg held up a hand to stop Freyja speaking. An impressively built woman in Valkyrie armour butted in, thumping a fist into her palm for emphasis.

'It's Scold!' Lotta gasped. 'She's back in Asgard!'

'Who's Scold?' Marta hissed.

Whetstone leaned towards his mum. 'She used to lead the Valkyries, before Glinting-Fire took over. A bit shouty.'

In the vision, Freyr appeared behind Freyja's shoulder. He said something which made the Gods laugh.

The Vikings in Drott shifted; Whetstone could hear a few angry mutters. The vision disappeared.

Glinting-Fire opened her arms. 'But we are here. We knew what was coming and we can protect you.'

'We don't need your protection,' bellowed Pjorn the Pig Wrestler, making Whetstone jump. Pjorn staggered forward, shaking off those who were holding him up.

Glinting-Fire shrugged. 'Fine. Let me show you what happens to those who refuse our help.' She pointed at the man and let out a sharp whistle.

Marta threw her arms around Whetstone as the air was filled with whispering black feathers. A flock of ravens descended on Pjorn, plucking the protesting man out of the crowd. They lifted him high into the air before carrying him over the walls of Drott and, with a final shout from Pjorn, dropping him into the outstretched hand of a Frost Giant. Whetstone closed his eyes as the crowd gasped. Crunching followed and the sound of someone being sick. With a quiet rustling, the ravens returned to the village, perching on the roofs, their bright green eyes watching the remaining Vikings.

Glinting-Fire smiled. 'Anyone else?'

'What's the price for your *protection*?' Heads in a range of pointy helmets turned to look as Lotta forcibly elbowed her way forward.

'What are you doing?' Whetstone hissed. He wiggled, but the press of Vikings was so tight he could hardly move. Marta's arms stiffened around him, holding him back. 'We need to make a plan!'

'Someone has got to save Midgard, and I guess it's going to be me,' Lotta announced, reaching the front of the crowd. The Vikings shuffled away; no one wanted to get too close in case Glinting-Fire set more ravens on her. The girl's brown face almost glowed with determination.

'Oh no, she's being a *Hero*,' Whetstone muttered, cringing.

Glinting-Fire peered down at the trainee Valkyrie, the tattoos on her face screwing up in disgust. 'Oh, it's you. I had hoped you were dead.'

Flay stepped out of the semicircle of Valkyries behind Glinting-Fire. 'The worlds have been opened, Brings-A-Lot-Of-Warts-And-Verrucas. You lost.'

Flee joined her sister. 'Yeah – loser.'

Lotta sniffed. 'Feeling better, Flee?'

'Yes, no thanks to your friend Freyja.' Flee tossed her plaits. 'Her spell finally wore off.'

Lotta puffed out her chest. 'Shame, I think I preferred you that way.'

Whetstone slipped out of his mother's grip and wiggled away. 'Where are you going?' Marta whispered as Whetstone squeezed through the crowd to try and reach Lotta before she did something *Heroic*.

Lotta pulled her shield up her arm. 'Glinting-Fire, I challenge you to a duel for command of the Valkyries.'

Whetstone shoved his way forward, his palms sweaty. If she got hurt, it would be his fault – he had told Lotta her plans were rubbish, so now she was going in without one.

Glinting-Fire slid out of her saddle and jumped down on to the platform. She stared down her nose at Lotta. 'We are offering these people a chance at life. Do you, a disgraced trainee Valkyrie who never made it past Class Three, really think you can offer them anything better?'

Lotta lifted her chin. 'Better than your trickery! You only gained power over the Valkyries through Loki's magic.'

Glinting-Fire's eyes narrowed. 'You're nothing without him.'

'Indeed.' A voice, which made Whetstone stumble in fear, echoed around the buildings in Drott. 'It's a good thing I'm here then.'

Vikings screamed as an enormous inky dragon appeared over the village walls, its outstretched wings plunging the village into darkness. Whetstone braced himself against the panicking Vikings, now desperate to escape the circling dragon. But the exits were all blocked by Glinting-Fire's Valkyries. Babies wailed; men fell to their knees in terror. Whetstone was shoved to and fro in the madness. From somewhere behind him, he could hear his mum calling his name. Whetstone ducked his head and used the chaos to wiggle forward. A cold giggle cut through the commotion. Fingers of ice crept up Whetstone's spine – he recognized that sound.

The Helhest dragon perched on the village walls, flapping its wings for balance, its thick talons digging into the wood and thatch. It bent its neck low over the Vikings, Loki and Hel, sliding down to land next to Glinting-Fire.

A shudder rippled through the Vikings. They fell silent as the Queen of the Dead surveyed them, the scent of decay wafting from her skin and clothes. The top half of her face was human; the bottom a grinning skull filled with needle teeth. She put her hands on her hips to look down at Lotta. 'I should've guessed you'd be here making trouble.'

Lotta's sword slid out of its scabbard with a scrape of metal. 'Remember this, Hel?' Silver drops ran along the notched

169

blade. 'It destroyed your Helhest last time – I wonder what would happen if I hit you with it?'

Hel's eyes crinkled with glee. She waved a hand and the Helhest dragon reared up on its back legs, its wings stretching out across the walls of Drott to form a dome, cutting the village off from the outside world. Someone in the crowd screamed as Loki threw a handful of green sparks into the air. They hung there, illuminating the space with an eerie light.

'Just in case you were thinking of going anywhere, Lotta.' Hel giggled. 'I want to see what Glinting-Fire's going to do to you.'

Lotta's face tightened in the silvery light of her sword.

'You have no power here, little

girl.' Hel smirked. 'You're all alone.'

'No, she's not.' Whetstone shouldered his way through the front row, using the bag as a battering ram.

Hel clapped her hands. 'He's here too! Your *Hero* – how sweet.'

The Vikings of Drott turned to each other. Whetstone could hear a few of them whispering.

Marta began to push her way forward. Grimnir followed, poking people out of the way with his stick.

Whetstone felt heat creep into his cheeks. 'Why do people keep saying it like that? I *am* a Hero.'

'Oh yes, the fearsome Rhett the Bone-Breaker, wasn't it?' Flay chortled. She jumped off the platform and snatched the bag out of Whetstone's arms to rummage inside it. 'Go on, put your helmet on and show everyone how Heroic you can be.'

Whetstone glared at her. 'What are you going to do, Flay? Bat your eyelashes at me again?'

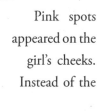

Pink spots appeared on the girl's cheeks. Instead of the

helmet, Flay pulled the cup out of the bag. It pivoted on her palm, taking in the watching Vikings.

'Ooh, an audience!' it preened. 'I would like to present – a poem:

> *There once was a young lad from Drott,*
> *Who everyone thought was a clot . . .*

'If you're not going to be helpful, be quiet!' Whetstone hissed, shoving it back into the bag.

'I think a Champion of Valhalla is exactly what these people need,' Loki said, opening his arms wide. 'Why don't you come up here and show them what you can do?'

Whetstone felt his face burn.

'What would you like to do first – defeat a Frost Giant or save a damsel in distress?' Loki's face creased into a sneer. 'Oh, I forgot. You're not very good at either of those things, are you, Whetstone?'

'*Whetstone?*' Whispers rippled through the crowd. '*That was Whetstone?*'

'Leave him alone, you bully!' Marta burst out of the crowd, Grimnir behind her.

'Lovely to see you again, Marta,' Loki sneered, giving the woman a small bow. 'I hope your return to Midgard was all you dreamed it would be.'

Marta's face curved into a snarl. She took a step forward, the mirror shard clutched in her hand. 'You lying, cheating—'

Hel rolled her eyes. She waved her skeleton hand and Marta

vanished with a *pop*. In her place was a frantically squeaking white mouse, the knife lying on the ground beside it. 'That's enough of that.' Hel examined her nails. 'Some people need to learn their manners, don't they, Daddy?'

Loki smiled, his scars twisting his lips. 'Certainly.'

Whetstone slowly picked up the mouse, who was trying to lift the knife in her tiny paws. He peered at her. 'Mum?' She scuttled back and forth along his arm, squeaking loudly.

Grimnir leaned on his staff. 'Does anyone mind if I take a seat? My legs aren't as young as they used to be.'

Without taking her eyes off Whetstone and Lotta, Glinting-Fire waved a hand and a green-eyed Valkyrie led the old man to one side.

'This is your mighty army, is it, Whetstone?' Loki laughed, jumping down from the platform. 'A rubbish Valkyrie, your mother and an old man. How fearsome.'

Whetstone clenched his jaw, grinding his teeth. Lotta pressed the mirror shard into his hand; he could feel the strips of cloth Marta had used to make its handle rough against his skin. The mouse scrambled up to his shoulder.

'Do you want to make any other futile displays of Heroism? Or shall we get on with choosing the first applicants for Camp Blood Claw?' Glinting-Fire took her clipboard out of one of the horse's saddlebags.

'Camp Blood Claw?' Lotta gestured at the trapped Vikings. 'Tell them the truth. What are you going to do with them?'

On the platform, Glinting-Fire smiled. She turned back to the watching Vikings. 'All we ask in return for our protection is that you serve us. We cannot save everyone, and that is why you must prove yourselves worthy. Only the strongest, the most obedient, the best warriors can be saved. If you are lucky enough to become servants of the Valkyries, then we will protect you from the monsters of the Nine Worlds. If you do not take this offer, I'm sure the Giants will find a use for you.'

Someone whispered, '*Sausages.*'

'Your choice is clear,' Glinting-Fire continued. 'With us, you have the chance of happy, long lives. Without us – Giant food.'

'You don't have to listen to them!' Whetstone cried desperately, turning to the crowd. The mouse's whiskers tickled his neck. 'There is another way. Loki has a magic harp – if we find that, we can put everything back the way it was before.'

Loki laughed. 'I think it's a bit late for that, don't you?'

Glinting-Fire turned on Whetstone with a snarl. The boy flinched – he had never been the focus of Glinting-Fire's attention before. The Valkyrie Leader might be no taller than him, but her fierceness radiated out several inches from her body like a particularly vicious halo. 'I have seen the best Heroes that Midgard has to offer,' she growled, her clipboard clenched in her hand. 'Warriors so terrifying it would make your hair drop out. Go home, little boy. You are no Hero, and you have no place here.'

'He's a better Hero than you are a Valkyrie!' Lotta cried.

'You're a freak, Brings-A-Lot-Of-Scrapes-And-Grazes.' Glinting-Fire focused on the girl. 'You are unfit to be called a

Valkyrie, and you will. Be. Dealt. With.'

'I'm unfit?!' Lotta threw her arms open. 'What is the main purpose of the Valkyries? To bring dead Heroes and warriors to Valhalla –'

At Glinting-Fire's signal, a pair of enchanted Valkyries swooped forward, grabbing Lotta by the arms. Flay wrestled her sword and shield from her.

'– building Odin's army to fight the Frost Giants at Ragnarok!' Lotta yelled as she struggled. 'Not to turn the humans into your slaves!'

Whetstone stepped forward to help her, but a second pair of Valkyries seized his arms. Whetstone thrashed, but their grip was too strong to break, the knife held uselessly in his hand. The mouse scampered down his arm, biting their fingers. A green-eyed Valkyrie flicked her away, flinging the mouse across the square where Grimnir caught her.

Glinting-Fire took a step back to survey the struggling Valkyrie. 'Don't worry, Lotta. We know how to fix you.'

'What are you going to do?' Lotta stared past Glinting-Fire to glower at the Queen of the Dead. 'Get Hel to do your dirty work and turn me into a mouse too?'

'Oh no, I think we can do better than that.' With a giggle, Hel jumped down to snatch Lotta's shield from Flay, the terrified Vikings flinching back at her approach.

'No!' Lotta lunged at Hel but was held back by the enchanted Valkyries. 'Get your bony fingers off my shield!'

Hel smirked. 'I'll do what I like, little girl.' The disc blazed in her skeleton hand. 'You really should take better care of your precious shield. Maybe I should put it somewhere safe for you?'

The silent crowd shuddered as two long strands of Helhest oozed down from the black dome covering the village. The tar-like creatures landed either side of Hel and took on human shapes, one looking like Lotta, the other Whetstone. Whetstone shivered as a sticky, black version of himself took the shield from Hel. Lotta yowled and thrashed like a wounded animal.

'What about over the door?' Hel waved a hand at the Great Hall and the Helhest stretched, lifting the shield up. 'No, maybe not. Perhaps over here?' Everyone turned as Hel skipped to the village well. She peeked inside. 'No, I know just the place.' Hel tapped a finger against where her lips should be. With a grin – although with her skeleton face, she couldn't really do anything else – Hel pointed through the open doors of the Great Hall at the shield rack.

'NO!' Lotta lurched forward again and was dragged back.

Whetstone kicked the girls who held him hard in the shins; they didn't react.

More Helhest dripped down from the dome. The Vikings recoiled in horror as it formed into a creeping black carpet, oozing into the Great Hall and returning with the shield rack, which glowed eerily with green ice.

'Don't, Hel! Please!' Lotta yelled, thrashing violently.

Hel carried the shield over to her father. 'Shall we do this together, Daddy?'

Loki placed one hand on the shield. It blazed with colour

before tendrils of green ice crept across its surface, meeting Hel's magic coming the other way. The colours grew dim. Unlike in Castle Utgard, green-black ice now covered the whole shield. The Vikings gasped.

With a cry, Lotta collapsed to the floor, the Valkyrie guards releasing her.

Whetstone wiggled, trying to see what was happening. 'Are you OK? Lotta? LOTTA!'

Glinting-Fire crossed her arms smugly. 'You might find your friend is a bit – *changed* now.'

Slowly Lotta got to her feet. She stood, her back ramrod straight. Whetstone peered into her eyes, his heart thudding

loudly in his ears. He could feel his fingers trembling against the knife. Rings of green covered the usual brown of Lotta's eyes. Lotta was gone.

'You could say, she's come round to our way of thinking,' Glinting-Fire continued.

Hel clapped her hands. 'Perfect.'

Flee looked at Lotta closely. 'Are you sure? We should test it.'

The corners of Glinting-Fire's lips curved up into a smile. She glanced at Whetstone. 'That is an excellent idea.'

Chapter Fifteen

Green-Eyed Zombie

Tucking his mother's knife into his belt, Whetstone rubbed his aching arms where the Valkyries had gripped him. He now stood alone at one end of the raised platform. At the other, Lotta waited motionlessly with a troop of Valkyries, her enchanted green eyes fixed on him. Whetstone shivered, wishing they had let him keep the falcon cloak. He could do with turning into a bird right now.

He straightened his tunic, acutely aware of the silently watching Vikings. All of Drott stood in the village square, their faces strange in the light of Loki's green crystals. Sounds outside the village were muffled by the Helhest dome, and the air was thick and heavy. Whetstone felt like he was in his own private nightmare world.

With shaking fingers, the boy fished inside the bag at his feet. The cup peered out. 'Where's Flay gone?' it asked. 'And why does Lotta look like she wants to kill you?'

'She's not Lotta any more,' Whetstone said around the lump in his throat. 'She's been Loki-ed.'

Loki, Glinting-Fire and Hel stood in conversation by

the shield rack, its green ice giving them a ghostly glow. Whetstone's eyes rested on Lotta's shield, balanced against the top of the wooden rack.

Glinting-Fire beckoned a tall Class Two Valkyrie with long dreadlocks to her. She muttered something and the girl nodded.

'Vikings of Drott!' Akrid turned to the silent crowd and raised her arms. 'You are privileged to witness a unique event. Our newest member –' she gestured at Lotta – 'Brings-A-Lot-Of-Scrapes-And-Grazes, will prove her dedication to the Rise of the Valkyries by defeating in single combat the human, and so-called Hero, Whetstone of Drott.'

Whetstone squeezed the cup in his hand, his palms sweaty. Single combat against Lotta. Again. And this time she wasn't armed with just a ladle.

The Vikings shifted at the sound of his name. Whetstone couldn't help but notice a number of them nudging each other and whispering. He thought he heard one say, 'That's Angrboda's boy . . .' Heat flushed through his body.

'You can't fight Lotta!' the cup squealed, wiggling out of Whetstone's grip and on to his platform. 'Valkyries are highly trained fighting machines. It's one of their six key skills!'

Whetstone shoved his hand back inside the bag, his fingers fumbling for the golden helmet. 'I don't know if I have much choice.'

'Oh dear.' The cup hopped sadly towards Grimnir, who had somehow acquired a folding chair and was sitting with his hands resting on top of his walking stick. The white mouse sat on his knee watching them with bright eyes. 'You're gonna get *mashed*.'

> *There once was a lad named Whetstone,*
> *Who everyone thought was a moan . . .*

'Thanks,' Whetstone muttered, sticking the helmet on his head.

Flee strode forward and plopped a long-handled axe in his arms. 'Good luck, loser.'

Whetstone clutched it to his chest and stepped into the centre of the platform, swallowing his nerves. He was a Hero, warrior, Champion of Valhalla – he could do this. He had faced down Giants, wolves, sea monsters, and now – his best friend.

Stepping out of the troop of Valkyries, Lotta prowled forward, silver beads running along the sword she held out in front of her.

Whetstone hefted the axe in both hands; he had forgotten how heavy these things were. He didn't want to hurt Lotta, but if he could knock her over, it might give him enough time to get away. He could still get the harp and fix things, he thought desperately. It couldn't end like this.

Lotta spun, her sword whizzing towards his head. Instinctively Whetstone lifted his axe to stop the blow. With a crash, the weapons met, sending vibrations up and down Whetstone's arms and making his hands tingle. As Lotta rebounded, Whetstone swung the axe, trying to keep her off balance. Lotta danced out of the way. Whetstone twisted his head trying to see where she was going, but the helmet slipped so only one eye was lined up with the eyeholes.

'Witness what happens to those who defy us,' Glinting-Fire announced to the silently watching Vikings. 'This is what passes for a Hero these days – this pathetic boy.'

Whetstone felt heat rise in his face. Inside his helmet, sweat trickled down the side of his neck. He couldn't do this any more. He was fed up with pretending to be something he wasn't. Whetstone tugged the helmet off his head.

'Now finish him off!' Glinting-Fire commanded.

Something heavy slammed into Whetstone from behind, knocking the axe and helmet from his grasp. Whetstone fell forward on to his knees, his fingers scrabbling to find a weapon. An arm wrapped around his neck from behind.

As Whetstone's vision filled with stars, a voice hissed in his ear, 'What are you doing? You almost hit me!'

Whetstone jerked in surprise. 'Lotta?' he choked. 'You're all right!'

'Loki shouldn't have let Hel get involved. Her magic doesn't work properly on me.' Lotta released him, giving Whetstone a shove so that he sprawled on the floor.

'But, your eyes –'

Lotta shrugged, holding her sword in front of her. 'I just feel kind of tingly. I think Hel's magic is blocking Loki's from reaching me.'

Lotta rocked from foot to foot as Whetstone climbed to his feet. 'You tricked her?' he said in amazement.

Lotta grinned. 'You really are massively unobservant, aren't you? You didn't notice when Flay was impersonating me, and you didn't notice that I wasn't really enchanted.' She winked.

'But –'

'We've just got to make it look good until I can get to the shields. I think I can break Loki's ice.' She waggled her sword, the silver droplets running along the blade.

'Then the harp?'

'The harp.' Lotta nodded, raising her sword.

Whetstone snatched up his axe and ducked away from Lotta. Loki and Hel moved out of the way as he skidded across the platform, dust trailing in his wake. He landed in a crouch in front of the shields, breathing hard.

Lotta fixed her green eyes on him, circling. Whetstone held his position as suddenly the girl spun towards him. The boy dived sideways as, with a double-handed blow, Lotta smacked her glowing sword into the shield rack. The sword bounced off without leaving a mark.

'Oh dear.' Hel laughed. 'You missed!'

'Loki's a Fire Giant,' Whetstone wheezed, standing up, his axe left at his feet. 'Only Giant magic can break his spell.'

'And you tell me this now!' Lotta hissed at him wide-eyed.

'I thought you knew – Flay told me when she was pretending to be you!'

Hel tipped her head, her black-and-white hair falling across her face. 'What's going on? Keep fighting!'

'Something made with Giant magic,' Whetstone muttered, fumbling at his belt. 'Like this!' He produced his mother's knife.

'From Loki's mirror-door!' Lotta rolled her shoulders. 'I really hope you're right about this.' She hefted her sword. 'I'll distract them – you free the shields!' With a smile on her face, Lotta turned to face the Queen of the Dead. 'Hey, Hel! I've got something for you!'

Sticking the knife between his teeth, Whetstone started scrambling up the slippery ice covering the Valkyrie shields.

In a blur of white, Marta the Mouse shot across the platform and vanished up Loki's trouser leg. The man yelped and jumped about as the mouse bit him on the knee.

In an almighty overarm throw, Lotta launched her sword squarely at Hel's face. Hel reacted instinctively, blasting a dark fireball towards Lotta. The fireball hit the sword, knocking it out of the air and turning the blade black. It landed with a sizzle on the rough platform.

'You, boy!' Glinting-Fire shoved Hel and Loki out of the way. 'Get away from the shields. Valkyries – stop him!' Flee and Flay produced their swords.

185

'Too late!' Lotta called as Whetstone reached the top of the shield rack. He held the knife aloft for a moment, before plunging it into the green ice. With a terrible splintering, fractures spread out across the shield rack, green ice flaking and falling away as the spell was broken by the knife. The scent of mint filled the air.

Around the square, Valkyries started to stumble as the magic controlling them weakened. A few staggered towards the platform, reaching for their shields. Flee and Flay glanced at each other, lowering their swords in horror.

'No! Loki, fix it!' Glinting-Fire stomped forward. She turned, looking for the Trickster. 'Loki!'

The man had vanished. Marta sat washing her whiskers alone on the platform.

'You're all on your own, Teeth-As-Clean-As-Glinting-Fire.' Lotta pointed at the tattooed Valkyrie. 'Where are your friends now?'

'You've ruined everything, you worm.' Glinting-Fire unsheathed her sword, pointing it straight at Lotta. 'You and that boy have been holding us back from the beginning.' The sword point followed Lotta as the Valkyries circled. 'Under my leadership, the Valkyries would have ascended to new heights. You could have joined us.'

Lotta put her hands on her hips. 'I would never join you.'

With a snarl, Glinting-Fire swung her blade at the girl. Lotta ducked but was too slow; the sword caught the edge of her helmet, knocking it off. It rolled across the platform with a hollow clatter, sending Marta scampering away.

Grabbing Lotta's shield, Whetstone slid down from the rack, kicking other shields free as he went. Valkyries surged forward to collect them.

'The time of the old Gods is over.' Glinting-Fire prowled closer. 'Under Loki and me, new Gods will rise.'

'You think you're a God?' Lotta spluttered, dodging another blow. 'Why can't you just be who you are?'

The woman lowered her sword for a moment. 'What I am is not enough! Everything I have achieved is through dedication and sacrifice. I have proved myself time and time again, and yet Odin chose the pathetic Scold to lead the Valkyries! It is time for *my* reward, and I will be greater than them all!' With a savage lunge, Glinting-Fire sent Lotta sprawling.

'Catch!' Whetstone skidded Lotta's shield across the platform, but Glinting-Fire kicked it away before Lotta could reach it.

'No sword, no shield – what sort of fighter are you?' Glinting-Fire taunted.

Lotta looked Glinting-Fire in the eye. The woman recoiled from her gaze. 'I. Am. A. Valkyrie.' Lotta slowly got to her feet. 'Being a Valkyrie is the promise I make, every day, to serve Odin and uphold the Valkyrie code.' Lotta's eyes never left Glinting-Fire's face. The woman stumbled back as Lotta advanced. 'It's not something that you can trick or force people into being. It's not a magic spell or an easy way to get power. Being a Valkyrie comes from inside me, and some days it's really tough, and sometimes I get it wrong.' Her eyes flicked to Whetstone, who grinned. 'But being a Valkyrie is who I am, and it isn't something you, or anyone else, can take away from me.'

Akrid joined Lotta in facing down the former Valkyrie Leader, her own shield now securely back on her arm, all traces of green vanishing from her brown eyes. 'Lotta's right.

Being a Valkyrie is a promise we chose to keep, and you have chosen to break that promise.'

Other Valkyries approached, nodding. Glinting-Fire's mouth opened and closed noiselessly, her eyes flicking from side to side as she was quickly surrounded by heavily armed and very angry Valkyries.

Lotta crossed her arms. 'Drop your weapon, Glinting-Fire. It's all over.'

Seeing no way to escape, the woman opened her hand. Her sword landed with a clang and Lotta kicked it off the platform.

'Your plan failed, Glinting-Fire. We *will* stop Loki, and we *will* free the Gods.'

'And when they do –' Akrid pointed at Glinting-Fire, Flee and Flay with her sword – 'you three will return to Asgard to face trial for breaking the Valkyrie code.'

The twins and Glinting-Fire were swiftly encircled by a ring of weapons.

'It was all Glinting-Fire,' Flee spluttered, dropping her own sword.

'We couldn't stop her,' Flay wailed as the three of them were dragged away under armed guard. 'We were on your side all along – honestly!'

Aware of all the watching Vikings, Whetstone carried Lotta's shield across the platform to her. 'That was amazing.' He grinned.

Pulling back her black puffs, Lotta smiled at Whetstone. 'Thanks.' She ran her fingers lovingly over the splintery shield.

'We make a pretty good team, when you're paying attention.'

'It wasn't just me.' Whetstone turned to the Queen of the Dead. 'We couldn't have done it without you, Hel.'

Skeletal fingers clenched into fists; Hel threw back her head and screamed. Above them, the Helhest dome trembled.

As if a spell had been broken, the Vikings, who had been silently watching the Valkyries, started to lose control, fighting and flailing in their desperation to get away from the vibrating Helhest. With a sucking noise, which was almost drowned out by shouts and wails, the dome peeled away from the walls reforming back into the inky dragon. Sunlight poured into the village square, dazzling Vikings and Valkyries alike.

Whetstone and Lotta threw themselves against the platform as the dragon extended a scaly arm, snatching up Hel in its claws. With a massive leap, the dragon took to the skies, turning only to spit blue-black fire at the Vikings and set the roof of the Great Hall alight.

'This is the end!' shouted Norm the Merciless. 'Save yourselves!'

Vikings stampeded towards the exits. Over the walls of the village, Giants loomed, waiting for the villagers with hungry expressions.

Lotta rolled over to grab Whetstone's shoulder. 'You have to stop them, otherwise they're all Giant food!'

'How?' Whetstone looked around in despair. 'Why me?'

Lotta looked into his eyes. 'Because you're a Hero, and they need a Hero right now.'

Whetstone took a deep breath and stood up. 'Hey!' The

190

boy waved his arms, trying to attract the attention of the Vikings. Who ignored him.

Lotta scampered across the platform to pick up Glinting-Fire's discarded megaphone.

'**OI!**'

Her magically amplified voice echoed across the village square. The Vikings paused in surprise.

'Listen to him.' She pointed at Whetstone.

'Stop!' Whetstone panted, climbing back up the shield rack for extra height. 'We have to work together, otherwise we're all going to be eaten!'

'But what can we do? We're just ordinary people, not Heroes,' yelped a woman clutching a crying toddler.

Whetstone pushed his shoulders back. Behind him the thatched roof of the Great Hall crackled with dark flames that gave off no heat. 'I know you all remember me. I used to live here with Angrboda. She was my foster mother. You –' Whetstone pointed at a woman in the crowd in a patterned headscarf – 'you're Unn. You made the best bread rolls. Not that I ever got many. And you, Rollo –' Whetstone pointed at a boy a bit older than himself – 'you tried to push me in the village well on my seventh birthday. Although come to think of it, it probably wasn't my seventh birthday as I don't think Loki or Angrboda know when my actual birthday is.' Whetstone was aware he was gabbling, but he couldn't seem to stop the words coming out of his mouth.

'Get to the point,' whispered Lotta.

Whetstone swallowed. 'The point is, I'm nothing special.

I'm an ordinary person, just like you. But if I can stand up to Loki and his evil plans, so can you. Help us!'

'How?' called a voice.

Whetstone set his jaw. 'I need to find Loki's magic harp.'

'Well, father is with Angrboda. So the harp is probably there too.'

Whetstone almost slipped off the shield rack in shock. 'Vali!'

Vali shoved his hand through his moss-streaked hair, the crowd parting around him like a stone in a river.

'You got out of Asgard then,' Lotta said with a laugh. 'And you're helping – *us*?'

Vali shuffled forward. 'Father left me in Helheim with skull-face for months. Can you imagine what that was like?'

Lotta wrinkled her nose.

'If the walls stay open, she stays here, so –' Vali smiled and the crack that ran down the side of his face twisted. 'Besides, I thought you wanted all the help you could get?'

Whetstone nodded. He jumped down from the shield rack and turned to the Vikings. 'We need to get to Angrboda's kennels. That'll be where the harp is. If I can reach that, I can close the walls again and put everything right.'

Puffing, Olaf the Sweaty climbed up on to the platform. He pointed at Whetstone. 'Wet-pants is right. We can't just let them take over Midgard without a fight.'

Akrid wiped down her helmet before sticking it back on her head. 'We need to take Glinting-Fire back to Asgard.' The other Valkyries nodded. 'And we need you to sort out this mess before we can do that. We'll take care of Hel and the Helhest.' The Valkyries unsheathed their swords.

'Don't let it touch you,' Vali warned. 'It feeds on Viking spirits.'

Akrid nodded.

Whetstone turned back to the Vikings. 'Frost Giants might be strong, but humans are faster. Keep moving and you're harder to catch.'

'And find some armour to stop the Elf-shot hitting you,' Lotta advised. 'Things aren't the same as when they first arrived – you know what to expect now.'

Unn, who made the best bread rolls in the village, waved her rolling pin in the air. 'Right! Let's show them how we do things in DROTT!'

'Meet by the gates – bring any armour or weapons you can find,' Rollo added.

Akrid lifted her sword. 'Valhalla Forever!'

'Valhalla Forever!' the Valkyries and Vikings cheered, flooding out of the village square.

'Let's get rid of that black sticky stuff!' yelled Rollo.

'We're going on a Giant hunt – we're gonna catch a big one!' screamed the woman with the toddler.

Whetstone caught Lotta's eye and grinned. They clambered down from the platform to join Vali as the square cleared, leaving Grimnir standing alone.

The old man leaned on his walking stick. 'Well said.'

Lotta pointed a finger. 'Wait a minute – that's a false beard!'

The man smiled, unhooking the fake white beard from over his own, actual beard.

As Whetstone watched, Grimnir straightened up until he was no longer hunched over with age. Now a tall, broad-shouldered man with tanned skin, he pulled an eyepatch out of his pocket to cover his one missing eye.

'Odin!' Lotta quavered. 'Er – Allfather, Spear Shaker, Terrifying One-Eyed Chief –'

'Should we kneel?' Whetstone whispered to Lotta as two ravens swooped around the man, whipping his cloak up before perching on top of the staff. One of them eyed the white mouse sitting on the man's shoulder curiously.

'But –' Lotta wobbled, still staring at the Chief of the Gods – 'How did you get here? I thought Loki sent you to Jotunheim?'

The man stroked one of the ravens, who ruffled his feathers. 'He did, but when Loki opened the walls, he brought me here too.'

Vali crossed his arms with a laugh.

The cup hopped out from under Odin's cloak and bopped towards Whetstone.

'Nice one. I was sure you were going to die.'

Whetstone laughed. 'Me too.'

'But if you've been

194

here all along, why did you make us do all that?!' Lotta spluttered. 'You could've stopped Loki at any time!'

Odin's beard twitched into a smile. 'But then you wouldn't have learned that you were capable of doing it yourselves.'

Lotta's mouth opened and closed, her nose twitching. 'That's incredibly frustrating!'

Odin smiled. Blue lightning crackled around the village square, putting out the flames on the roof of the Great Hall and clearing the muggy air.

'How are you doing that?' Whetstone spluttered as goosebumps rose on his arms. 'I thought only a Giant could affect another Giant's magic.'

Odin tipped his head, half of his face falling into shadow. 'I was not born with magic. To earn my powers, I hung from Yggdrasil for nine days and nine nights, a spear piercing my side. A sacrifice of myself to myself. In doing so, I learned the secrets of the dead. Hel's magic is no mystery to me.'

Whetstone and Lotta looked at each other, agog.

'Which reminds me . . .' Odin gently placed the white mouse on the ground. Blue lights twinkled and Marta reappeared.

'Mum!'

Marta folded Whetstone into a hug. 'I'm so proud of you!'

'The job is only half done,' Odin cautioned. 'Glinting-Fire's plan is finished, but you still need to stop Loki.' The Allfather walked over to the platform to collect the golden helmet. 'Will you be needing this?'

Whetstone disentangled himself from his mother and

scratched his neck. 'I think I'm fine without it, thanks. You can keep the cup too. Take it back to Frigg.'

'But how can I make up more poems about you if I don't see what you get up to?' the cup complained.

Whetstone smiled. 'I'm sure you'll come up with something.'

'Right –' Lotta sheathed her scorched sword – 'let's get out there and finish this.'

Chapter Sixteen

Together Again

The Vikings and Valkyries stormed out of Drott, waving axes, spears and one very surprised live chicken. The landscape flickered crazily around them, mountain ranges, forests and deserts appearing and disappearing. Feet thudded through snow and flowers, and across gritty soil.

Directly in front of them waited Hel with her Helhest army. Hundreds of inky, oozing soldiers formed a ring around the village. Behind them, Hel stood on a platform, her teeth bared, a spear clutched in each hand.

Filling the air with terrifying battle cries, Valkyries threw themselves at the Helhest, swords and shields clashing.

'Odin Owns You All!' screamed one, hacking at Hel's soldiers.

'Death or Glory!' screamed another.

'I don't even like the colour green!' wailed a third.

Nidhogg the dragon looped around the fight, blowing fireballs and smoke rings.

Behind Hel waited the Giants. Elves chattered from boulders and the few remaining trees, Elf-shot raining down

on anyone unfortunate enough to venture too close.

Marta led the Viking horde, having found a helmet and chainmail shirt somewhere. She brandished her mirror-knife. 'Guess who's out of the cage now!' she bellowed at Skrymir, her white hair streaming out behind her. She darted through the Helhest line to stab her knife into the Giant's foot.

Behind her came the rest of the Vikings, slashing and hacking at anything they could reach.

With an icy blast, the worlds changed. Snow from Jotunheim smacked into the swirling mists of Niflheim. Icicles grew at strange angles as the freezing winds blew, giving the trees and boulders icy teeth and claws. Valkyries and Helhest battled in the gaps

in the fog, Giants stomping down on the tiny figures beneath them.

Whetstone, Lotta and Vali ducked through the murk, Vali's grey skin blending in with the fog, the sounds of battle ringing all around them.

'This is impossible,' Whetstone panted, dodging a cloud of Elf-shot. 'We'll never get past this lot.'

Vali smirked. 'I have an idea.' He stuck two fingers in his mouth and gave a piercing whistle. A loud bark answered him. In a cloud of grey fur, a wolf the size of a house leaped through the Giants and Helhest to land in front of Whetstone and Lotta. A blood-red tongue lolled out of his gaping jaws and clouds of dog breath wafted over them. Vikings shrieked at the sight of him.

Fenrir sniffed the air, then lowered his head to give Whetstone a huge lick before rolling over for his tummy to be scratched.

'He's missed you!' Lotta cooed as Whetstone scraped dribble off his face.

'You big baby,' Vali muttered, rubbing the huge wolf's ears.

'He's still definitely my favourite of all your relatives,' Lotta said with a smile.

'Fenrir,' Vali said into the wolf's ear, 'take us to your mum's kennels. Can you do that?'

The wolf gave an answering yip, which made Whetstone's head ring, before rolling on to his paws and crouching low to the ground.

'Up we get.' Vali pulled himself on to the wolf's back using

Fenrir's fur as hand- and footholds.

Lotta bit the inside of her lip. 'After you.'

Whetstone grinned. 'At least it's not a cat.'

❋

Things were quieter outside what was left of Angrboda's kennels. Snow fell gently, muffling the sounds of battle and blotting out any footsteps.

Fenrir trotted to a halt and Lotta slid down from the wolf's back. 'Are you sure this is the right place?' She looked around at the flattened buildings and snow-covered landscape. 'There's nothing left.'

Vali and Whetstone climbed down to join her. Shivering, Whetstone wrapped his arms around himself. He gazed at the ruins of what had once been his home. 'This is it. Where is everyone?' Unease churned in Whetstone's stomach. Maybe he was wrong, and the harp wasn't here after all?

With the grating sound of stone on stone, Vali crossed his arms.

Fenrir cocked his head, his mouth open, panting.

Faint musical notes drifted past on the breeze, filling the air with a soft, warm sound. Lotta grabbed Whetstone's arm, her fingers pinching his white skin. 'The harp!'

His heart thudding loudly in his ears, Whetstone held his finger to his lips. He led Lotta and Vali around the shattered wolf kennels, following the harp music. They paused at the top of a ridge – the music was coming from somewhere in the trees below them.

Whetstone caught Lotta's eye and pressed his lips together. Wherever the harp was, Loki was bound to be there too. He half wished he had brought the golden helmet to hide behind, but Lotta was right: being a Hero or a Valkyrie was down to a choice that you made, not something that you wore.

'Let's go.' Lotta pulled her shield higher up her arm and crept into the trees. 'Together we can face whatever Loki has planned.'

'Yeah, a Valkyrie with superpowers, a Hero who can't fight and a Troll. We're practically unstoppable,' Vali muttered.

Lotta rolled her eyes. 'Optimistic as ever, Vali.'

Picking their way through the trees, the children followed the music towards a sheltered hollow, Vali's stone feet leaving deep tracks in the snow. They paused as a golden glow appeared between the trees. The music was louder here. Whetstone held his breath and eased down a branch to see.

Shining with a gentle light, the harp Whetstone had been searching for sat alone on a tree stump, the wind brushing through its silver strings and filling the air with music.

Whetstone released the branch and went to take a step forward, but Lotta put out a hand to stop him. 'Is this a trap? It feels really trappy.'

They both glanced at Vali, who sighed. 'You're going to have to decide if you trust me or not.'

Whetstone shrugged. 'There's no point in Loki tricking me now – he's already got everything he wanted.' The boy turned back to the harp. 'Maybe I could just take it?'

Lotta raised an eyebrow but lowered her arm.

Leaving Lotta and Vali in the trees, Whetstone moved forward, his feet crunching through the frost. The harp was just as remarkable as Whetstone had remembered. About as long as his forearm and softly rounded with a carved dragon head snarling over three strings. He had held it once, many months ago, when Loki had hidden it in the branches of Yggdrasil.

With trembling fingers, Whetstone stretched out and pressed his hand against the harp strings. The music fell silent, and the snow stopped falling.

'What happened?' Lotta whispered, her voice loud in the sudden silence. 'Are the worlds still shifting?' She peered up into the sky: the horizon was streaked with pink as the sun tried to poke through grey clouds.

'The harp was designed to move the person who held it between worlds,' Vali reminded them. 'Father twisted the magic to bring all the different worlds here. Now that the music has stopped, the worlds should return to their rightful places.'

'So, this is still Midgard?' Lotta dug her toe into the snow. Far away a bird started to sing.

'As long as we're not stuck in Helheim, I don't care,' replied Vali, crossing his arms.

'Of course it's not Helheim,' Lotta replied with a sniff. 'There are no birds in Helheim.'

Keeping his fingers pressed to the strings, Whetstone used his other hand to pick up the smooth harp frame. It felt surprisingly light, the strings twinkling with a silvery light. He turned back to the others, smiling. 'I got it!'

'But how are you going to keep it?'

The smile froze on Whetstone's face. Standing behind Lotta was Loki, a knife at her throat. 'How apt. We all started this together, and now we'll all finish it.'

Lotta stomped down hard, trying to find Loki's toes. The man flinched but kept hold of her. Vali scowled at his father, his hands shoved deep into his pockets.

Whetstone straightened, peering up at the Trickster. 'It's over, Loki. I've got the Skera Harp and I'm going to return it to the Dwarves. This all ends today.' He held Loki's gaze.

Abruptly the man released Lotta. She stumbled forward to join Whetstone, rubbing at her neck and coughing.

'Fine,' shrugged the Trickster. 'Do it.'

Whetstone goggled; even Vali looked up in surprise. 'What?' Whetstone spluttered.

The knife in Loki's hand vanished in a flash of green light. 'Return the harp. Break the curse. Go on. I'll even show you which chord to play to lead you to the Dwarves.'

Whetstone glanced at Lotta, bewildered. 'What? Why?'

Beside his father, Vali shifted, silently watching them.

Loki smiled. 'Because you don't want to. Not really.' He took a step forward.

Whetstone's hands tightened on the harp.

The Trickster's smile widened. 'Do you actually *know* what happens if you break the curse?'

Whetstone's skin tingled, flushing hot and cold. What was Loki talking about? 'I get my parents back. We can all be on Midgard together again. And you –' he nodded at Loki – 'can't mix up the worlds any more.'

From the other side of the hollow, a human-sized Angrboda appeared through the trees, her Frost Giant skin bright blue against the white snow. 'Well, I suppose you're half right.'

Whetstone and Lotta shuffled deeper into the hollow, trying to keep both Loki and Angrboda in sight at the same time.

'Hello, Vali,' Angrboda said in a falsely sweet voice. 'I hear you've been spending quality time with your half-sister.'

Whetstone saw a muscle twitch in Vali's stone jaw.

'Tell us, then,' Lotta growled. 'What happens when Whetstone breaks the curse?'

Loki's mouth curled up at the corners. 'Everything goes

back to the moment the curse took hold. So, yes, you will be back with your parents. Twelve years ago. None of this will have happened.'

Whetstone's face scrunched up in confusion. Lotta sucked in a breath.

'You'll never become a Hero,' Loki continued. 'Never visit Asgard, or Helheim, or Jotunheim. You'll never defeat a dragon or save a magical cup. And you two –' he gestured at Whetstone and Lotta – 'will never meet.'

The two friends turned to look at each other, wide-eyed. Lotta blinked first. 'He's lying.'

'Am I?'

'Is he?' Whetstone staggered a step. He felt like he was falling. Everything he had been working towards had shifted. It had never occurred to him that by breaking the curse, he might never see Lotta again.

'Or,' Loki continued, 'you can leave things as they are.' He shrugged. 'You're here on Midgard. Your parents are here on Midgard. I'm sure we could find a quiet little pocket somewhere for you to set up home.'

Whetstone twitched.

Lotta narrowed her eyes. 'What about the Gods in Asgard – are you going to let them out?'

'No. I don't think so. They'll all stay safely tucked away where they can't hurt anyone.'

Lotta's hands clenched into fists. 'We stopped Glinting-Fire.'

'Yes, well done.'

Angrboda leaned against a tree, her purple hair dappled

in the sunlight. 'Whetstone, you're giving up a lot for your parents. Two people who you hardly know.'

Loki nodded. 'Your friend, your place in Valhalla. No one will tell stories of your adventures or sing songs about your exploits.'

'He doesn't care about that stuff,' Lotta huffed, crossing her arms.

Loki watched her with dark eyes. 'Doesn't he?' He focused on Whetstone. 'You'd just be another boring human, spending your days growing cabbages and dreaming of the adventures you'd never have.'

Whetstone took a step back.

'But, you *would* have your parents back, and family is *so* important,' Loki continued. Vali gave a hollow laugh.

'Where are the Fire Giants?' Lotta opened her arms. 'If *family is so important*, where is yours? You're a Fire Giant, and I know you opened Muspell because I saw the volcanos – so where are they? Don't they like you or something?'

Loki pouted. Vali's forehead wrinkled in thought.

Lotta nudged Whetstone. 'Come on, we've got a harp to return.'

Whetstone backed away, the harp still clutched in his arms. He could feel the power in the harp strings thrumming against his chest. 'Maybe I could just separate the worlds and release the Gods, but not give the harp back to the Dwarves?' he muttered. Lotta glared at him. 'Then I definitely wouldn't go back in time. Everything would just carry on from now.'

Lotta shook her head. 'It wouldn't work. Remember the riddle?'

The final part of the riddle danced through Whetstone's mind.

The pieces must all be sought, and joined once more as one,
None shall be whole until Loki's crime is undone.

Undone. There was no getting round it. No tricks. He had to undo Loki's crime, not try and wiggle around it. His life wouldn't be whole until the Skera Harp was returned to the Dwarves.

Whetstone flexed his fingers over the strings. 'How do I reach the Dwarves?'

Loki licked his scarred lips, his eyes fixed on the harp.

Lotta slid into position next to Whetstone, her sword in her hands. 'Don't come any closer – just tell him. He's made his choice.'

'Don't do it, Whetstone,' Angrboda warned. 'You won't be able to control the magic. Get it wrong and you'll be smeared across the Nine Worlds.'

'Different note combinations will take you to different worlds.' Vali twisted a knife between his fingers. 'It's pretty simple. Don't let go of the frame, and keep trying till you find it—'

Loki turned on his son with a growl.

Vali backed away. 'You dragged me along on this stupid quest in the first place, so don't be surprised if I figured stuff out for myself on the way!'

'You brat!' Angrboda snarled. 'You might be stone, but I

can still make your life a misery.'

'Do it then,' Vali challenged her, the knife stilling in his stone fingers. 'What can you do that Hel can't?'

Lotta sheathed her sword and grabbed hold of the harp frame. Angrboda stalked forward, momentarily blocking Loki's view of Whetstone, her attention focused on Vali.

'Play something!' Vali yelled.

A chord appeared under Whetstone's fingers. The boy and girl vanished, pale fingers snatching at Whetstone's tunic as they went.

Chapter Seventeen

Through the Worlds

Wind whistled past Whetstone's ears. The world spun, like he was flying and falling all at once. He kept his eyes tight shut. He could feel Lotta breathing hard next to him, her brown fingers trapped between the harp and his chest. When he managed to open his eyes, colours swirled, making him feel even more sick.

'Wheeeee!' Lotta yelled.

'I cannot believe you're enjoying this!' Whetstone ground out between his teeth.

Just when he thought he couldn't bear it any longer, the whistling stopped and his feet hit the ground with a thump. Lotta crashed into him, knocking him on to his side.

The ground was black and curiously warm; grit scratched at his cheek. Whetstone rolled on to his back and felt sweat break out all over his body. He swallowed down the nausea and opened his eyes. In a gap between boiling sooty clouds hung the green-and-blue world of Midgard. Whetstone groaned and ran his hand over his face, leaving streaks of ash behind. Looking at his home world from this angle would make anyone feel sick.

'Not bad.' Lotta reached down to help him to his feet. 'This is Muspell,' she explained. 'Land of the Fire Giants.'

Whetstone struggled to catch his breath. He clutched his ribs, looking around. He was standing in a vast plain, everything within it made of the same gritty black rock. In the distance a volcano spat red sparks into the boiling sky. Hearing the crunch of footsteps, Whetstone wobbled around to see Loki walking towards them.

'How did you get here?' Lotta spluttered. She picked up the harp – which had landed, thankfully undamaged, at Whetstone's feet – and pressed it into the boy's arms.

'Thanks for the lift home, Whetstone.' The man dusted ash off his clothes. 'Although I have to admit, I haven't visited my brothers and sisters for such a long time.'

Whetstone blinked – the heat and bad landing was making him feel very peculiar. 'Of course.' He tried to avoid looking at Midgard, hanging sideways in the sky, as it made him feel like he was about to fall over. 'You're a Fire Giant. You come from here.'

Loki nodded, looking around. 'What a dump.' Against the horizon, a volcano shuddered. Loki held out his hand to Whetstone. 'Give me the harp.'

Whetstone's fingers closed around the smooth wood. 'No way.' His ribs ached; every breath felt like agony.

Loki laughed. 'I can keep this up all day, Whetstone, but you don't look too good. Humans aren't meant to travel between worlds.'

'Maybe not, but *I* am –' Lotta narrowed her eyes – 'and I'm going to get him to Svartalfheim if it's the last thing I do.'

'It will be the last thing you do if he returns the harp,' Loki warned. 'You'd better say goodbye now – there won't be time later.'

Whetstone glanced at Lotta and gulped. The Valkyrie was glaring at Loki, but her fingers twisted together nervously. 'Shut up. You're wrong,' she muttered.

The grit beneath their feet started to tremble – grains of

sand coming together, piling up into enormous feet, ankles and legs.

'The Fire Giants are coming!' Lotta yelled over the rumbling.

'We have to go, before they fully form,' Loki shouted over the rumbling, as pebbles and small stones joined the sand. 'Send us somewhere else. Play the harp.' The sandy toes next to Whetstone wiggled before being encased in tall black boots. 'I said: play the harp!'

Whetstone stumbled backwards, tripping over the feet of another enormous black statue. Red light appeared in cracks as the man twisted and stretched.

Loki grabbed the harp, finally succeeding in pulling it from Whetstone's sweat-slippery fingers. The man held the harp aloft in triumph, but before he could touch the strings, an enormous black hand dropped on to his shoulder, knocking the harp out of his grasp. Lotta dived after it as Loki pulled at the hand, unable to free himself.

'Loki! I should've known it was you,' said the figure in a jovial voice.

Loki slumped. He plastered a smile on his face. 'Sutr.'

With a whoosh that filled Whetstone's eyes with grit, other people formed. They were now surrounded by a group of stony figures, each twice the size of a human. Fire Giants.

Lotta slammed the harp into Whetstone's chest, making him gasp. 'Let's go,' she hissed.

Loki's face went rigid. 'How's Mum?'

'You don't write. You don't visit,' said a tall, thin woman

with sharp teeth. 'What sort of son are you?' Pouting, she crossed her arms and tapped her long fingers on her upper arm. Hel obviously got her looks from her grandmother.

Whetstone wrapped his fingers around the harp frame. Lotta was right: they needed to get out of here. But every second they got closer to the Dwarves was one second closer to maybe never seeing Lotta again. He looked up at Loki and Sutr. 'Wait, you're brothers?'

Lotta huffed in frustration.

Sutr laughed. 'I know. Hard to believe, isn't it? I'm much better-looking.'

Lotta pulled Whetstone out of the way as with a ripple of crimson light, Sutr and the other Giants changed. In a swirl of red cloak, Sutr reappeared as a fashionably dressed Viking man with gleaming black onyx skin. The other Fire Giants turned into group of Viking men and women. Sutr rubbed a hand across his carefully trimmed goatee.

'To be changeable is the nature of fire,' he said to Whetstone's stunned expression. 'Loki isn't the only shapeshifter in the family.'

Whetstone gulped and nodded. His ribs throbbed and the heat radiating off the Fire Giants made him feel dizzy. Lotta gripped his arm, holding him upright. Whetstone hugged the harp against his chest. The only things that seemed real were the wooden harp and Lotta's hand on his arm.

'Well, it's been lovely meeting you all, but we should go,' Lotta began, drawing Whetstone away. 'I'm sure Loki would love to stay and catch up though.'

Loki's mother pushed her way to the front. She now appeared to be a bright-eyed Viking woman with sharp cheekbones and a collection of sewing needles threaded through her apron. She squeezed an uncomfortable-looking Loki in a hug. 'Look at you! You're so thin – you must eat.'

'I opened the walls – why didn't you come out if you missed me so much?' Loki asked, escaping his mother's clutches.

Despite his dizziness, Whetstone pricked up his ears.

Sutr laughed again, a deep, warm sound. 'At Ragnarok we will rise and burn the Nine Worlds. But it's not yet Ragnarok, so we can wait. *You* need to learn patience.'

Lotta laughed. Whetstone couldn't help but grin. Loki barely managed to wait twelve years for the harp strings.

'What are you smirking at?' Loki turned on Whetstone, his fingers flexing. Green sparks leaped between them.

Lotta jiggled Whetstone's arm. 'Time to finish this. Loki, enjoy your family reunion.'

Whetstone's fingers found the strings; new notes emerged at the same time as a blast of green fire from Loki's hands.

The boy and girl disappeared.

New ground materialized under Whetstone's feet; he stumbled, gasping. The harp slid out of his grasp as he fell face first into a patch of green grass. The greenest grass he had ever seen, certainly from this close. He heard Lotta land somewhere nearby with a splash. The boy pushed himself up on to his hands and knees, reaching for the golden harp. A wave of nausea passed over him.

Swallowing hard, Whetstone glanced around. He was in a forest, but the colours were all wrong. The grass was too green, the trees were too brown, and the flowers were so bright they hurt his eyes. A stream tinkled past, too-blue water swirling past Lotta's knees as she sat up, her hair dripping.

'Wrong way,' Lotta explained, wringing water out of her hair. 'This is Alfheim.'

A chattering came from above him. Still on his hands and knees, Whetstone looked up to see a row of silver faces with pointy ears peering at him between the leaves. 'Uh-oh.'

Ignoring the Elves, Whetstone sank down on to the grass; his skin felt hot and cold. Flashes of darkness kept appearing in front of his eyes, and his chest ached. Lotta waded out of the stream to join him, water pouring out of her armour.

'Lotta,' Whetstone said thickly, 'I don't think I can do this. I feel really weird.'

Lotta stuck her hands under his armpits to try and lift him back to his feet. 'You are getting that harp back to the Dwarves if I have to drag you there myself,' she panted as Whetstone slipped down.

Whetstone shook his head. 'Maybe you should do it. Take the harp.' He pushed the instrument into her hands.

Lotta pushed it back. 'No way. You have to do it.' Her face softened. 'It's your quest, Whetstone. It always was. This is up to you.'

Whetstone closed his eyes to avoid her determined expression, all the worries Loki had stirred up inside him burbling to the surface. 'What if Loki wasn't lying? What if this is it? I don't want to forget all about you. You're my best friend.'

Lotta crouched down beside him. 'Whetstone, if this is it – if we get zapped back in time and forget everything – it will still have been worth it.' She took his hand. 'You know what? I'm glad I picked *you* up instead of a *real* Hero. No one else could've done the things you've done. You've been the best Hero, the best fake-musician –' Whetstone couldn't help but grin – 'and the best friend I could ever have asked for. And no one – not Loki, not the cursed harp strings – can take that away from us.'

Whetstone squeezed Lotta's hand.

Lotta grinned. 'I tell you what, if it all goes wrong, I'll meet you in that stable in Krud in twelve years' time. We can do it all over again!'

Whetstone giggled. After a couple of false starts, he got to his knees. 'Thanks, Lotta. And just so you know, your plans are pretty good. I'm sorry I didn't pay more attention to them.'

She thumped him on the arm, nearly knocking him down again. 'I knew it!'

Whetstone cradled the harp in his arms. 'One more try?'

Lotta smiled. 'That's the plan.'

From beneath the boy's fingers another chord rang out and the green forest vanished.

❊

Whetstone opened his eyes. He was lying in a dark and dripping cave, just like the one Loki had shown him in that vision all those months ago. 'Svartalfheim.' He rolled on to

218

his hands and knees to retch, but his stomach was empty. Whetstone felt dizzy, his head throbbed, but the harp was still clutched tightly in his hand. 'Lotta, we're here.' His voice echoed back to him.

The boy got to his feet, cracking his skull on the low ceiling. He'd obviously grown since Loki's vision, or maybe Loki had made the ceilings taller then. Lights flashed in front of his eyes and he was aware of something watching him from the darkness. Some *things*. Whetstone stumbled forward in a crouch, hoping to find the Dwarves, or at least somewhere he could stand upright. His head swam, the cave walls swirling around him.

'Lotta? Where are you?'

A pair of warm hands caught him as he fell. A short man with a long beard and pointy ears said something in a language

Whetstone didn't understand, but he nodded anyway. Other bearded and pointy-eared faces crowded in around him. Whetstone held out the harp. 'Here, the Skera Harp. I brought it back.'

Strong fingers tugged it from his hands. There was some muffled conversation before music filled the narrow space, a tune Whetstone half thought he recognized.

'That's nice,' he muttered, his eyes closing. Maybe everything would make sense when he woke up.

There was the sound of heavy boots running towards him followed by a kerfuffle. Dwarves moved around him. Whetstone tried to open his eyes as a hand shook his shoulder. A pair of concerned brown eyes peered into his face. 'Whetstone?'

Whetstone felt himself slipping away. 'If I got it wrong, I'm sorry. Goodbye, Lotta.'

Chapter Eighteen

That's How to Be a Hero!

Whetstone groaned. His head throbbed. He opened one eye and a ceiling swung into place above him. He stared at it dumbly for a few seconds: it was brown with thatch and a large spiderweb hung in one corner. It looked both familiar and strange. Swirling images filled his head: peculiar landscapes, blue-skinned Giants, volcanos and ravens. A simple thatched ceiling didn't seem to fit in somehow.

After managing to open his other eye, Whetstone sat up and swung his legs off the bed. His head thumped, nearly making him lie back down again. He looked around curiously. He was in an empty and unfamiliar longhouse. A loom sat in one corner, half-finished fabric tight across its frame. Weapons and tools hung from the walls. The sound of birdsong and a hint of a blue sky poked in through cracks in the door.

Holding his head, Whetstone stumbled outside. The air was frosty and burned in his lungs. Icy mud creaked under his bare feet. A woman with the whitest hair he had ever seen was hanging out some washing. He tottered towards her. At the sound of Whetstone's footsteps, she turned. But before she could speak, a loud voice echoed across the landscape.

'He's awake!'

Quicker than he could blink, Whetstone was surrounded by a swarm of odd-looking people – some trying to shake his hand, others trying to lift him into the air. Whetstone goggled as a beautiful woman with warm brown skin and golden threads woven into her black twists swooped down to give him a kiss on both cheeks.

A short, suntanned man with stained teeth and spectacular tattoos bobbed out of the crowd to point at him. 'Look – it's Rhett-stone!'

The boy almost fell over as a large man with a red beard and heavy hammer threw an arm around his shoulders. 'I always knew he could do it. I told you, didn't I, Tyr?'

An equally muscular man nodded.

'What's going on?' Whetstone panted as he tried to wiggle free.

The beautiful woman pulled Whetstone away. 'Give him some air,' she instructed, her voice cutting through the gabbling crowd. 'He's been through a lot, poor boy.' She looked into Whetstone's pale face. 'What's the last thing you remember?'

The crowd fell silent; Whetstone could almost feel them listening. He closed his eyes, ignoring their curious expressions. 'It was dark. I fell – I think.' He opened his eyes. 'Did I hit my head?'

The beautiful woman raised her eyebrows. 'Go on.'

Whetstone took a few steps away; it was hard to think with everyone staring at him. 'There was music, and green light? I was travelling.'

The woman nodded; she straightened up. 'I knew it. Loki hit him with something before he was trapped in Muspell. Probably a memory spell.'

'Loki?' Whetstone almost laughed. 'What are you on about? What would Loki want with me? I'm . . . nobody . . . important.' He looked from one colourful face to another. 'Am I?'

The woman guided Whetstone to a nearby bench. 'Don't rush it. You'll remember in time.'

'We should feast – it's not every day a human saves the Nine Worlds!' cried the man brandishing his hammer.

'Who are you talking about? And watch what you do with

that hammer!' Whetstone gulped. The people around him were becoming more familiar, if no less odd. Glowing lights flickered around them. Whetstone rubbed his eyes.

A tall man with an eyepatch nodded. 'Excellent suggestion. We could all do with a break from the Valkyrie trials.' One of his ravens soared up into the sky.

Whetstone watched the bird go. 'A party?' He turned back to the woman. 'You're – Freyja? Didn't you have a birthday party?'

The woman smiled.

With a flicker of rainbow lights, the Bifrost Bridge appeared next to the longhouse, making Whetstone gasp. A line of Valkyries, now back in their usual armour, marched out of it bearing cups, jugs of mead and even a couple of benches. More scarred and tattooed Heroes followed, and even a group of musicians in feathery hats. One man was bowed double under a long battle horn.

'I don't have to wear the outfit this time, do I?' Whetstone asked, horrified.

'It's all coming back to you then?' Freyja asked with a laugh. She drifted away as Whetstone's parents approached. Marta took his hand.

Behind his beard, Hod looked serious. He leaned over to mutter in Whetstone's ear, 'Hey, what's a cow's favourite party game? Moo-sical chairs!'

Whetstone groaned. 'Your jokes are no better.'

'I've got more.' Hod grinned.

Marta squeezed Whetstone's fingers with a smile. 'And we've got plenty of time to hear them.'

'Let's have a boast battle – about Whetstone the Bold!' the man with the red beard shouted as the Valkyries handed out drinks and the musicians set up their instruments.

Freyr yelped in excitement, his golden eyes glowing. 'We'll all have a turn! Me first!' He gestured to the musicians, who finished readying their instruments and started picking out a bouncing rhythm.

Freyr walked in a circle, pushing Gods and Valkyries into position. Whetstone found himself in the front row in between his

parents. His dad gave his shoulder a squeeze.

'One verse each. Yes, even you, Thor,' Freyr instructed, pointing at the red-bearded man. 'Let's hear those rhymes!' Stepping into the centre, he raised his arms and began.

> *Freyja's party went with a bang!*
> *Loki's back, but where's the rest of his gang?*

Someone whooped; people started clapping in time to the music. Whetstone couldn't help but grin.

> *Chased out of Asgard; it's time to go*
> *Find the Giants – don't be slow.*

Freyr bobbed back into the circle. Freyja tossed her dark twists and stepped forward, taking up the song.

> *A boy and a girl in a castle full of Giants;*
> *Lotta's been kidnapped – let's start a riot!*
> *Flay's in disguise – it's all part of the plan*
> *To find out your secrets – resist if you can.*

She blew a kiss at Whetstone before stepping back. Whetstone felt his cheeks grow hot. His dad grinned at his discomfort. Thor tossed his hammer into the air; several people ducked.

> *They found the cage, but his mum is gone.*
> *She's in Midgard – Loki can't be wrong.*

Now the race is on to get the last string.
Back to Drott. That's the –

Tyr whispered in his ear, 'Thing.'

Thing!

The Valkyrie Leader, Scold, was next. She grinned, her armour gleaming in the sunlight. She held out her hands.

Wait!
This is great!
Now give me a minute to get things straight.

The Valkyries whooped and cheered.

The wolf-mad Bogey is really a Giant!

Scold continued.

Let's sneak in: Shhh, be quiet.
So many ravens; they're Valkyries too.
Glinting-Fire's in Drott – she's looking for you!

Whetstone gulped, the swirling images in his head starting to settle into memories. Escaping Skrymir's castle, Angrboda turning into a Frost Giant, Glinting-Fire trapping everyone in Drott . . .

Vali twisted a knife between his stony fingers; the cup hopped about on his shoulder.

> *Father fixed the harp; the worlds are mashed up.*
> *Giants, dragons, Helhest, and one gobby cup!*

The cup twirled on his shoulder and sang:

> *Trapped by Valkyries; it's a big mess!*
> *Got to free the shields – no time to rest!*

Stepping out of the group of Valkyries, Akrid shook back her dreadlocks.

> *With Marta's magic knife, the Valkyries are freed!*
> *Loki's spell is broken – he won't be pleased.*
> *Found the harp, thanks to Vali . . .*

She pointed at the tall boy. Whetstone could've sworn he saw a hint of a blush in Vali's stone cheeks.

> *Cross through the worlds – don't be shabby!*

Freyr danced forward again, leading a cheer.

> *Whetstone,*
> *He's come home,*
> *And this time, he's not alone!*

228

Odin's low voice reverberated around the gathering,

Break the curse, but is it the end?
Twelve years lost? Forget your friend?

The crowd parted and Whetstone spotted someone he hadn't realized he had been waiting to see. 'Lotta!' He moved towards her.

Her brown face scrunched up into a big grin. 'I TOLD YOU SO!' she bellowed, marching forward. '*That's* how to be a Hero!'

Odin stepped between them. 'Three cheers for Whetstone the Bold, saviour of the Nine Worlds and OFFICIAL HERO OF VALHALLA!!'

The crowd cheered and whooped. Whetstone grinned at Lotta as she rolled her eyes at him.

The musicians shifted the music into a dance. With the boast battle over, the Gods began to drift away in search of more drinks and other entertainments.

Whetstone inspected his friend critically. 'Are you wearing new armour? What's that badge for?'

Lotta thumped her breastplate. 'Pretty good, huh? It's because I'm a CLASS TWO now!' Behind them, Akrid polished her own Class Two badge with her sleeve.

'Well, if anyone deserves it, you do.'

'Hear, hear!' came Scold's voice.

Whetstone yelped as Lotta squeezed him in an armour-plated hug. 'I never said thank you, you know. For bringing me to Asgard in the first place,' he panted, rubbing his side; his ribs still ached from his trips across the Nine Worlds. 'If I hadn't met you, I would never have become a Hero, or found my parents.'

'Shut up.' Lotta whacked him on the shoulder. 'I won't hang out with you if you're going to be soppy,' she added with a grin.

'So that's it? Now the curse is broken,' Whetstone asked, 'it's all over?'

Odin brushed past them, a raven with a pickled onion in its beak balancing on his shoulder. 'Don't say that. There will always be more adventures. It's not Ragnarok yet.' He joined in as Freyr lead a conga line of Gods around the longhouse. 'La la la la la – hey! La la la la la – HEY!'

The cup bopped through the frosty grass, followed noiselessly by Vali. 'No one wants to hear my poem,' it complained. 'And I came up with it specially. I think I've summed up everything very elegantly.'

'There's a first time for everything,' Vali muttered, sticking his hands in his pockets. The cup blew a loud raspberry.

Whetstone stooped down to pick up the cup. 'Go on then.'

'Really?' The cup squinted at him. 'You never wanted to hear my poems before.'

Whetstone glanced at Lotta and grinned. 'I have a feeling this one is going to be a good one.'

The cup stood up proudly, winter sunshine glinting off its metal body. It cleared its throat and recited loudly:

He travelled across the Nine Worlds,
Flying and falling all in a whirl.
He won and he lost,
There's always a cost,
When you cross paths with Valkyrie girls!

'Perfect!' Whetstone laughed.

Keep reading for more fun
in the Nine Worlds!

Recipe from Skrymir's Feast

Want to eat like a Giant? Try this recipe for Spiced Oat Cakes. Whetstone has adapted the recipe for human-sized tummies!

> 225g ~~2 buckets~~ of porridge oats
> 110g ~~1 bucket~~ of unsalted butter
> 55g ~~3 trees~~ of chopped dried apricots,
>   apples ~~or humans~~ *No HUMANS!*
> 4 *TBSP* ~~1 beehive~~ of runny honey,
>   ~~leave the bees in for extra crunch!~~
> 1 *TSP* ~~An eggcup full~~ of ground cinnamon

1. Ask an adult for help and remember to wash your hands
2. Preheat oven to 180 Celsius
3. In a large saucepan, slowly melt the butter over a low heat
4. Remove from the heat
5. Stir in the oats, dried fruit, ~~humans~~ and honey until well mixed. *Do NOT ADD ANY HUMANS!*
6. Spoon dollops of the mixture onto a greased baking tray and flatten slightly. *FORM INTO HUMAN SHAPES FOR THAT AUTHENTIC GIANT'S FEAST TOUCH - YUCK!*
7. Bake in the oven for 10–12 minutes or until golden
8. Gently lift cakes onto a wire rack and leave to cool
9. Eat while toasting your friends and threatening your enemies!

Giant Name Generator

If you want to fit in with the Giants,
you'll need a new Giant name.
Use the table below to help.

First letter of your last name:

Angr or **A**sta	**N**al or **N**ott
Bjoll or **B**lizars	**O**svald or **O**ffa
Cheg or **C**ak	**P**rim or **P**etr
Dofri or **D**ana	**Q**akr or **Q**uari
Ern or **E**dna	**R**icka or **R**holf
Fala or **F**rosti	**S**mog or **S**kaldi
Gurt or **G**rimm	**T**off or **T**hrym
Herg or **H**elbringr	**U**ndr or **U**ri
Imr or **I**mmoni	**V**og or **V**algerd
Jord or **J**orm	**W**yland or **W**andea
Kaif or **K**ala	**X**avi or **X**air
Liek or **L**aufrey	**Y**ma or **Y**oan
Mjoll or **M**orn	**Z**indr or **Z**an

Birth Month = Home World

January, May, September	Jotunheim (Frost Giant)
February, June, October	Muspell (Fire Giant)
March, July, November	Midgard (Sea Giant)
April August, December	Helheim (Undead Giant!)

Colour of your socks = Favourite drinking song

Red, blue or yellow	*There was a Sad Giant with Only One Leg*
Black, grey or white	*I feel like smashing Asgard tonight*
Green, purple or orange	*I'm dreaming of a White Midwinter*
Striped, patterned or no socks!	*Om-Pah! Om-Pah! (Giants forever!)*

Asgard Crisis Flow Chart

Lotta has invented this handy flowchart to help solve any future problems which might occur in Asgard.

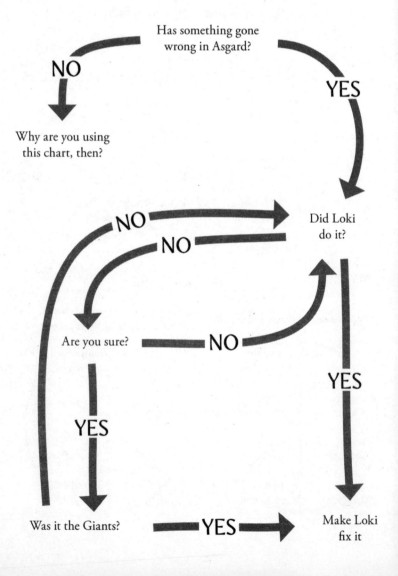

Design a Contest of Champions

The Heroes of Valhalla want a new Contest of Champions. Help them create a new contest by closing your eyes and randomly placing your finger on one option from each section.

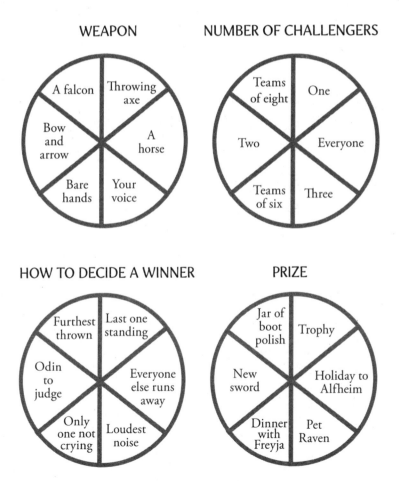

WEAPON

- A falcon
- Throwing axe
- Bow and arrow
- A horse
- Bare hands
- Your voice

NUMBER OF CHALLENGERS

- Teams of eight
- One
- Two
- Everyone
- Teams of six
- Three

HOW TO DECIDE A WINNER

- Furthest thrown
- Last one standing
- Odin to judge
- Everyone else runs away
- Only one not crying
- Loudest noise

PRIZE

- Jar of boot polish
- Trophy
- New sword
- Holiday to Alfheim
- Dinner with Freyja
- Pet Raven

The Creation of the Nine Worlds, or why the Gods and Giants hate each other, as retold by Whetstone.

To start off there was nothing. Then one place that was all fiery appeared, and another place that was all icy came along, and in the middle, in between them, there was something called the Ginnunununugagap, wait that's not right. It's the Ginnungagagagap. The Ginnunigagap. I can't say it.

Anyway, in the gap place the ice turned into a giant. I think he was a giant, he might've been a God. Or just someone really tall. His name was Ymir, and he was really sweaty. He did so much sweating that his sweat turned into other people. That is properly sweaty. These definitely were Giants, or as I like to call them – armpit people.

Then a cow turns up, maybe she was in the ice too, I dunno. And she starts licking the ice and another man appears, his name is Bor. He marries one of the armpit people and has a son – Odin. Odin gets bored of there only being fire, ice, a cow and some armpit people, so he decides to create some actual worlds with proper people, and animals and shoes and stuff. So Odin kills Ymir (bit harsh as he hadn't really done anything except sweat out people and hang out in the Ginnunigappy place). Anyway, so Odin uses different bits of Ymir to make different worlds. His bones turn into mountains, his skull is the sky and his brains – yup brains – are clouds. Gross. But kind of cool too.

Odin gives one of these worlds to the Giants to say sorry for murdering their great-granddad and gives another world to the Dwarves, who just kind of turn up, and another world to the Elves and some other worlds to other people. Then he makes Asgard and lives there for ever and ever and ever and ever.

Somehow out of all this mess, Yggdrasil grows and holds up the worlds that Odin made. I dunno, maybe Odin had some giant tree seeds in his pocket or something. Oh, and all the humans are made out of driftwood. No seriously, go look it up.

And that's why the Frost Giants hate the Gods so much, because Odin murdered their great-great-great-great-granddad or something.

Seriously, Whetstone? This is the worst version of this story I have ever heard. - Lotta

Armpit people? You smell of armpits, Whetstone - Vali

Author's Note

In Norse mythology the Gods and Giants have a *complicated* relationship.

Everyone knows that at the end of time there will be the final battle, Ragnarok, between the Gods and Giants (or Jotuns to give them their proper name), but what happens before then? And why do they have such a troubled relationship to begin with?

Despite being bitter rivals, Gods and Giants have more in common than they would like to admit. It is even possible for Gods and Giants to marry and have children. Thor is one such example, his father, Odin, is a God but his mother, Jord, is a Giant. This doesn't seem to stop him beating up the Giants with his hammer at every opportunity. Odin is at least half Giant, and in the Norse creation story the Nine Worlds are even made of bits of Giant! The Giants are just as essential to the Nine Worlds as the Gods.

But the Giants aren't one unified group. There are many different types of Giant, and some of them aren't even all that giant! They range in size from the humongous, like the Giants Whetstone and Lotta meet, (or those in the story where Thor and Loki shelter in a Giant's glove believing it to be a cave), others are almost human-sized. There are Frost Giants, Fire Giants, Giants who live under the sea and even Giants in the Lands of Dead. Yes, Hel is a Giant. Don't tell her, her ego is big enough already.

Like all the creatures in the Nine Worlds, Giants can be helpful or harmful, but we will have to wait until Ragnarok to really see what they can do.

I have had the best time exploring the colourful and chaotic world of Norse mythology with Whetstone and Lotta, but I feel as though I have only just scratched the surface of these people and places. In fact, there is one world we have never set foot in at all, can you figure out which one? I hope you have enjoyed your travels around the Nine Worlds with us. I love seeing your art and reading your stories inspired by *How to be a Hero*. As Odin would say, 'Keep it up, it's not Ragnarok yet!'

Visit me at catweldon.co.uk or on twitter @weldoncat

Acknowledgements

As ever I need to say a *gigantic* thank you to lots of people who were instrumental in bringing *A Gathering of Giants* to life.

Firstly, my wonderful friends and family. In particular my husband, Steve, and our lovely children, Georgia and Immie, who are all endlessly enthusiastic and encouraging. Not forgetting our puppy, Floss, who keeps me on my toes by stealing everything in sight when I'm trying to write.

A big thank you to my mum, and to my dad who died in 1993. Without you indulging my endless trips to the museum I wouldn't know half as much as I do about history.

This book wouldn't exist without my lovely agent, Alice, who was the first person to see the potential in the series, and without whom none of this would have happened.

A Giant-sized thank you to the people at Macmillan Children's Books who have done so much make the *How to be a Hero* series a success. Especially Sim, Sabina, Sarah, and Cheyney. Thank you as well to all the people who have worked hard behind the scenes to make these books the best they could be.

How to be a Hero would be less colourful without the beautiful illustrations from Katie Kear. There were a few times when I laughed evilly wondering how in the Nine Worlds you were going to illustrate some of the things in these stories. Your Giants and sea monsters are second to none!

Thank you to all the schools who have invited me into

their classrooms to bang on about how brilliant the Vikings are! I loved every second, and I'm sorry about the toenails.

Writing a book can be a lonely experience, and I spent a lot of time talking to my computer so I guess I should probably say thank you, computer. You were a wonderful listener. I couldn't have done it without you.

About the Author

Cat Weldon writes funny books for children and is a little bit obsessed with Vikings. With an MA in Scriptwriting, and a background in children's theatre, Cat has also worked as an English and Drama teacher – and in lots of other jobs where she can talk while waving her hands around wildly.

Cat Weldon now lives in East Anglia with her husband, daughters, and collection of delinquent chickens.

Although she has a favourite cup, it has never once recited poetry to her.

About the Illustrator

Katie Kear is a British illustrator and has been creating artwork for as long as she can remember.

Katie has an illustration degree from the University of Gloucestershire and has worked with publishers including Pan Macmillan, Penguin Australia, Andersen Press and Hachette. She is always on the hunt for brilliant stories to illustrate.

In her spare time she loves drawing, adventures in nature, chocolate, stationery, the smell of cherries and finding new inspirational artists!